Throw the Cap

An April May Snow

Southern Paranormal Fiction Thriller

By

M. Scott Swanson

April May Snow Titles

Foolish Aspirations
Foolish Beliefs
Foolish Cravings
Foolish Desires
Foolish Expectations
Foolish Fantasies
Foolish Games
Foolish Haints

Prequel Series

Throw the Amulet

Throw the Bouquet

Throw the Cap

Throw the Dice

Throw the Elbow

Throw the Fastball

Throw the Gauntlet

Throw the Hissy

Never miss an April May Snow release.

Join the reader's club!

www.mscottswanson.com

"Good friends are hard to find, harder to leave and impossible to forget."

- G. Randolf

Chapter 1

I finish proofing my case study answers for the second time and lay my pencil down. Fifteen minutes of test time remain according to the digital clock behind Professor Rosenstein's desk.

Should I proof my answers for the third time? Maybe, but it's not part of the plan today. I'm only required to pass. I gave up the ghost on perfection ever since receiving my job offer from Master, Lloyd, and Johnson.

It's impossible to contain my self-satisfied grin. April May Snow has completed law school. I stand at the starting line of my spectacular new life.

My Keds rise off the freshly polished floor, making a sticking noise as I bounce my legs. I can't wait for Rosenstein to call time so I can turn in the completed exam from the last final of the capstone class of my third year of law school. Unless a future case of temporary insanity hits me, my days of formal education are officially complete.

Please don't misunderstand. The University of Alabama proved to be a blast. But I bet even heaven is a drag after the seventh year.

College has been more fun than my wildest dreams. Still, I need to begin making some serious money posthaste. The banks holding my student loans send me friendly letters and emails daily, reminding me they own a generous portion of my future earnings.

Knowing the banks' names are effectively written on my impending pay stubs for darn near perpetuity does not make me happy.

What does make me happy? The idea of my future career in Atlanta. I worked my tail off the last seven years to land a position with Atlanta's most prestigious law firm.

I glance over at my study buddy, Martin Culp. I raise my eyebrows to inquire how he feels he fared on the exam.

Martin holds his hand up, moving it from side to side as he feigns a yawn. Martin may sometimes be a goober, but he is my best friend and a fantastic study partner.

He favors me with a devilish grin and tips his hand up in front of his lips.

Drinks? Ugh. After completing the final exam of a three-year program, I suppose the proper etiquette would be to celebrate. With graduation in three days, my parents due in town, and the fact that I'm presently operating on only two hours of sleep from last night, I need to go home. I have two essential items on my current to-do list: clean my filthy apartment and take a nap.

Since I left my parents' home, my brothers continually tease me that I have been at a country club with an around-the-clock happy hour. I may resemble that remark. It wouldn't be too much of a stretch to claim that I have earned a double major in partying while enrolled in college. So, the last thing I should need is a drink, and even to the hardcore fun-seekers, noon might be too early to begin drinking.

I wink at Martin and give him a thumbs up.

Hey, don't judge me. This may be the last time I share a drink with my study partner, who excelled at reminding me when the next assignment was due.

Professor Rosenstein strides toward his podium. His slight build and hunched shoulders crunch his tall form inward, causing him to appear small and passive. His rich reddish-brown and gray hair curls into thick, unruly shocks.

If not for Rosenstein, I wouldn't be completing law school.

When I enrolled at Alabama, I planned to follow in the footsteps of my daddy, the engineer. By the end of my first year, I realized I couldn't hack all the math and science required for an engineering degree. I can *do* math and science with the best of them. But those two subjects require a tremendous amount of homework.

Homework really interfered with my underage drinking and partying.

Clearly, I needed a new major. I considered accounting for a hot minute but took too long to make up my mind, and all the classes filled up.

In his late twenties and thirties, Rosenstein excelled as a high-powered defense attorney in California. Looking for a better life balance— mainly to escape a messy divorce—Rosenstein accepted the position of assistant dean of the law school in his early forties.

This is all information he volunteered to us during his "wine tasting and non-fiction book club" nights. I'm proud to say I have received an invitation to this sought-after event every month since we first met.

It is highly unusual for a professor of his stature to instruct any undergraduate classes. Graduate instructors typically don't like mixing with the unwashed masses.

But Rosenstein insists on instructing one undergraduate class a year. He claims he prefers to interact with students before four years of political correctness has them regurgitating the clone-like dialect. It also allows him to recruit students he believes should consider a law career.

The semester of my great indecision, Rosenstein worked overtime to convince me I was a lawyer and, specifically, a litigator.

In retrospect, I must admit he hit the nail on the head. With each passing year and class, I am increasingly confident about my chosen profession.

It isn't like I had never considered law as a career before Rosenstein recruited me. After all, my uncle Howard Snow has a successful practice in my hometown of Guntersville, Alabama.

But without Rosenstein's insistence and affirmation, I would not have chosen a law career on my own. Why else would I select a profession requiring me to apply myself as much as I have in the six years since I decided? I mean, getting away from having to challenge myself was why I ditched engineering. Right?

I'm blitzed before Martin shows the slightest appearance of having a buzz. He is drinking beer, and I'm drinking red wine. I will master the technique of sipping my Merlot one of these days rather than downing it like shots.

"I'm going to call for a ride home and take a nap," I announce.

Martin tilts his head to the right. "C'mon, Snow. Don't wimp out on me. We got all night to celebrate."

"I will remind you for the hundredth time I only managed two hours of sleep last night. I've got to clean up my place before my parents get here. *And* I promised the queen bee, Breanna, that I would help the sorority decorate the house tomorrow." I narrow my eyes. "Besides, don't you have some girlfriend you need to hook up with?"

Martin is dating a cute sophomore by the name of Penny Trickett. I enjoy teasing him about the need to tuck her in at night after making sure she says her prayers.

I don't care one way or the other that there are five years between their ages since they are both adults. I only kid Martin about it since he is amusing to aggravate.

"She is in a tutoring session that lasts until ten," he says.

"She must be as dumb as a box of rocks if she needs a tutoring session that long. And here I thought you said she was smart. Besides dating you, of course."

"She is teaching the tutoring session."

Whoops. I blew that one. "As if."

"What do you care anyway?" Martin sulks.

I can't conceal my laugh. "Because you implied that I need to stay here as long as you're still drinking. There is no way I'm drinking with you any longer tonight. I've got important stuff to be attending to."

"Then invite me over to watch T.V. while you take your nap. I'll help you clean your place afterward."

My face twists in repulsion. "No way."

He shrugs. "I'll bring my own beer."

"Drink your beer in your own apartment."

"But there's nobody there. It's depressing to drink alone." He feigns a sad face.

Okay, his puppy dog eyes—he does make the most pathetically sad face—tug at my heart and my limited Southern social graces of hospitality.

Still, for being so bright, Martin can be incredibly stupid. "You'd be drinking alone at my place, too. I'll be in bed."

His eyes open wider. "You're really not going to let me come over?"

I giggle. "No, you idiot."

"Man, that's a sorry way to treat a friend."

Chapter 2

My stomach grumbles so loudly it wakes me. I check my circa 1999 clock: 7:00 p.m. No wonder I'm hungry.

I pad to my kitchen. As I exit my bedroom, I notice a man—thank goodness it's Martin—sprawled on my sofa as if he is dead.

Darn it. I forgot I told Martin he could come over.

The mini pyramid of beer cans on my cluttered Formica coffee table dissuades me from checking if he has been shot. He is sleeping off his beer.

I examine myself—basketball shorts and a sports bra. I consider grabbing a T-shirt, but it is just Martin. I could walk nude to the fridge, and Martin wouldn't notice. Besides, my sugar level is crashing quickly.

Foraging in my refrigerator, followed by my cupboard, is not as fruitful as I had hoped. Next week, I'm moving out of my apartment, and I have purposely let my food supplies dwindle. My logic was sound until now.

Great. That means I will have to drag myself back out of my apartment. I scan the kitchen and living room to ascertain the required minimum amount of cleaning needed before my family arrives. It isn't too bad.

Oh, who am I kidding? It is a pigsty, and that is before I get to the Prince Harry look-alike who is beer-snoring on my sofa.

I grab a stray T-shirt off the barstool in front of my counter and give it a quick sniff. Not lilac fresh, but not ripe. I pull the shirt on and rock Martin's shoulder with my hand. "Hey. You want to go get a burger?"

Martin sits up and wipes his hand roughly across his eyes. "I'm sorry. I didn't mean to fall asleep. What time is it?"

"About seven thirty. Are you hungry?"

"Okay. Bubba John's?" He grins as his eyes remain half hooded.

I was thinking about something a little more basic and a lot more conservative on the calories. Bubba John's specializes in fusion burger monstrosities. But hey, it might be the last time I ever eat a Bubba John's burger.

Bubba John's should rent golf carts. They would make a mint. A golf cart is the only way I will manage to get back to my apartment after dinner. I'm as full as a tick.

Nobody denies that Bubba John's caters to the male crowd, where quantity is equally as important as—or possibly more than—price. I'm not a guy, but I play one when I eat. It is impossible to resist a two-third-pound burger. Especially when it is topped with a half-pound of barbeque pork, three strips of bacon, and a dab of coleslaw, all held in place with a blanket of two slices of pepper jack cheese. All this and some French fries you don't need, for the student-friendly budget price of five dollars. It's a fantastic deal as long as you don't ponder the origin of the meat products in too great of detail.

I understand the concept that I only need to eat until I am satisfied. The problem is that—even though I have the ability to stop eating when I become full—I rarely possess the discipline to actually do it.

Martin recounts the entire final exam while waiting for our food to settle. It amazes me how efficiently Martin's mind retains the smallest detail.

Me, not so much. Not because I don't have a good memory. I do. It is that my interest button is sort of broken. There are a lot of things I don't care much about anymore.

"One thing is for sure. Old Rosenstein is going soft. His tests aren't half as difficult as they used to be."

"Maybe you're just twice as smart as you used to be."

Martin leans back and sighs as he considers my point. "Do you think so?"

I dab at the condensation ring my glass left on the table. "Nah." I break into a laugh as I watch his eyes narrow.

"I will not miss you busting my balls, Snow."

"Oh, you'll miss me."

"Honestly, I don't believe so."

I gain control of my laughter. "Are you still going up to DC?"

"I'm all set."

Martin's dream has always been to move to Washington, DC, and work in and around politics. I used to kid him that he would have been better served to attend an Ivy League school. Lord knows he is smart enough. I thought nobody up there would hire a kid from the U of A.

Apparently, yes. Last month, Representative Weber from the Fourth Congressional District offered Martin an internship.

"I hate to think that one of my friends is crossing over to the dark side."

"I'm not going to the dark side. I'm bringing the light to run all the cockroaches out. You watch. I'm going to bring respectability back to DC politics."

"At this stage, that would be a tall order for God."

Martin grins. "I certainly won't refuse divine assistance. It's about getting the job done, not receiving credit for the accomplishment."

Martin will need supernatural assistance. He is intelligent and capable with zero street smarts. There isn't a single scenario in my mind where Martin doesn't end up swallowed by that city of egomaniacs. Martin is too sweet and always desiring to work as a team. Still, I hold out hope that I'm wrong and he can attain his goal while remaining true to his lovely character.

"You'll have to call me occasionally. I want to hear you brag about how many cockroaches you've run out of DC."

Martin smiles, exposing the dimple in his right cheek. "I'll have my assistant call and check up on you in your corner office in Atlanta."

"That's big of you." I will miss Martin. I've never had to worry about how he will take what I say. We are both given to being wisecracks and are rarely judgmental with each other. I know it is a special relationship, and I already mourn the passing of our season together.

Yes, Martin, my best friend, is a man. No, it isn't as odd as you think that my closest friend happens to be a guy. I have two brothers and no sisters. Often, I feel more comfortable talking with guys rather than women, even my sisters from the sorority.

I have female friends. Still, I feel I often have to be guarded around them. Worrying about how they may take my jokes is exhausting. Not to mention, a few of my girlfriends seem to live for creating drama. I once loved drama, but I no longer have the energy for it.

I wonder who my friends will be in Atlanta. My eyelids droop. "What time is it?"

Martin and I reach for our phones simultaneously. "Hello, where did the time go? It's ten thirty," Martin says as his eyes open comically wide.

"Ooh. Penny's going to be mad at you." I shake my finger at him. "No sex for you."

"That's what she'll be saying on the phone. She'll change her mind once she sees me." He pushes back his chair and drops ten dollars on the table.

"Why? Do you have a Channing Tatum outfit in your car?" I set two fives under my glass.

"Funny. Believe it or not, some women find me attractive."

I feign confusion. "Really? Is this with the lights on or off?"

"Sticks and stones, Snow. I'll catch up with you tomorrow."

"See you later, Martin."

Watching my broad-shouldered friend exit the bar, I wonder if Penny knows how good she has it. She is quite the lucky girl to have a great guy already thinking about the long game with her by his side.

I guess it is fortunate for Martin, too. He is the marrying type. Another reason why the whole DC thing has never made sense to me. But you can only point out the obvious so many times to a friend before you begin to irritate them.

Martin is an intelligent guy. If he wants success badly enough, he will figure out how to have his dream job in politics and his perfect American family.

Me? I will head to Atlanta and become the most sought-after corporate litigator in the Southeast. Nah, make it in the country. Why put regional boundaries on my goals?

Chapter 3

My phone rings. I must have passed out on my sofa while watching *Lord of the Rings* for the thirtieth time.

I stare at the display and see *Martin*. "Hey, what's up?

"Penny never showed."

I would joke about the situation if it weren't for the near-panicked tone in his voice. "And she is not answering her phone?"

"No. She is not answering my texts, either."

Not good. Many men might forget their phones or allow their batteries to run down. Me? I would be more apt to leave a hand or a foot behind than leave my phone. If Penny isn't answering, she either doesn't want to talk to Martin or can't answer—not by her choice.

"I'm sure she just turned it off during the tutoring session and forgot to turn it back on."

"I don't think so. I think something is wrong. I think I need to call the police."

"Whoa. Slow your roll, Martin. What are you going to tell the police? Your girlfriend isn't taking your calls?"

"She could be lying in a ditch somewhere."

True. Penny could also be lying on her back somewhere.

Stop it, April. Penny hasn't given me any reason to think like that. "Have you gone to her house?"

"No."

It is a darn good thing Martin plans on making politics his career. He would stink as a prosecutor. "Martin, if you go by her house and her car is there, you can be assured everything is okay."

He exhales. "You're right. I should drive by and see if she is home. Her phone might be on the fritz. It's not that unusual. Right?"

I become dizzy as my patented danger radar tingles across my skin. What caused that?

"Phones nowadays are only good for two years, tops. I think Penny has had her phone for four years now." Martin continues to ramble.

Fudge. The last of the sleepy fuzz leaves me as I realize why my sixth sense has kicked into gear.

What if Penny is at a girlfriend's house, and they are having a "no guys" night? If Martin drives by her house and sees her car gone, he will go into a full-fledged panic, worrying that something has happened to her. To quote Martin, "Lying in a ditch somewhere." He will notify the police that she is in danger and missing. When Penny shows up the next day after spending the night at her friend's, she will crucify him for being overprotective.

A dark thought crosses my mind. What if Martin instead finds a matte black Silverado at Penny's? The truck Damien Owens, Penny's high school sweetheart, drives.

Yeah, the police will be getting a call in that scenario, too. A domestic disturbance call.

I click my nightstand lamp on and search for my sandals. "Hey, Martin, why don't you come by and pick me up? I'll ride with you."

"What? No. It's two in the morning."

"I don't mind."

"Don't be silly. I'll drive over there, check for Penny's car, and ring the doorbell to make sure she is okay. Like you said, her phone is probably on the fritz."

In my junior year of high school, I thought I was in love with Randy Leath. On the weekend of the annual Snow reunion, I told my parents I was too sick to attend. It was a ruse to get Randy and me some alone time for a heavy-petting session.

I had the excellent idea that Randy should park his car down the street at the convenience store and walk to my parents' lake house. That way, no nosy neighbors would know he was visiting me. Perhaps Damien Owens knows the same trick. What will happen if Martin knocks on Penny's door tonight and Damien opens the door?

That could get ugly quick. In that scenario, the police would have to deal with an even uglier domestic disturbance.

"I don't think waking your girlfriend at two in the morning will endear you to her."

"But how will I know she is okay?"

As I mentioned before, Martin would be an abject failure as a prosecutor. "Dude. If her car is there, take a walk around it. If you don't see any fresh dents, you know she wasn't in an accident and is home. Tada! Your girlfriend is safe and sound."

"That is why I call you. Thank you."

His comment brings a smile to my face and warms my insides. I'm glad I could put my friend's mind at ease. Still, I have the raging case of the tingles on my skin to consider. I just don't know if it is my usual nervous energy regarding my friend's plight or my psychic abilities waking up. "No worries. Are you sure you don't want me to ride with you?"

"No. I'm good. Besides, you've got that thing with Breanna at your sorority in the morning."

A wave of frustration crashes over me. Why couldn't I have told Breanna no? "Thanks for reminding me. You call, I make you feel better, and you make me feel worse. How does that work?"

"You forgot, didn't you?" I can hear the amusement in his voice.

"No. Yes. Man, I'm sick of decorating. I must have decorated for a hundred parties in the seven years I've been at this campus."

"Aw, come on. It's your last rite of passage. Imagine you're in jail and this is your last time to go before the parole board. Only the board is your sisters, and you only need to show them who the master is one more time before you earn your freedom forever."

There sure does seem to be a sudden flood of "the last time to" events lately. It is like a victory tour in my honor that I never requested.

"Thank you for being my conscience—I guess," I offer.

"No sweat."

"Text me and let me know everything is okay with Penny."

"I will. Try to get a couple of hours of sleep."

The tingling sensation in my skin does not subside after our discussion. Perhaps the feeling of impending doom has nothing to do with Martin. If they are of the psychic sort, my senses only indicate that *something* is about to happen. I only wish I knew what.

My stomach remains bubbly from the alcohol, and I decide I want some cheese crackers.

I sit in front of my TV, mindlessly shoving cheese crackers into my mouth. I'm watching some survival show where the people run around naked with bug bites all over their skin and their privates digitally blurred away.

I wait anxiously for Martin's text. Hopefully, Penny's vehicle is in her driveway.

It is odd she isn't taking Martin's call. That is what piques my anxiety. If I was supposed to meet my boyfriend and my phone quit working, I would, I don't know, maybe drive to his apartment and tell him my phone died?

But I don't know Penny that well. At best, my interaction with her is limited to a couple of awkward double dates. She seems a bit uncomfortable that Martin and I are such good friends.

The discomfort is mutual. Penny oscillates in her relationship with Martin. One week she seems overly clingy, and the next week she is too busy with her girlfriends and studies to get together with Martin for dinner.

Martin is "all in" when it comes to Penny. I am positive she does not have the same level of commitment. I can't pinpoint why I am so confident, but I feel her affection lacks intensity.

There is something problematic about hanging out with a man. I can never voice my concerns about any of his girlfriends unless he requests my opinion explicitly. Even then, it is dangerous at best to comment. If I were to agree that his girl did him wrong after she dumped him, it would put our friendship in future peril. There is always the possibility that they will make up later or—worse—marry.

Then what? I'm the friend who told him the woman he would die for is an egg-sucking dirty dog. It's tough to take that back and be invited to the wedding shower or the wedding.

I've stuffed at least another thousand unneeded calories into me when my phone finally beeps. "Penny's car is here. All good. Thanks!!"

That bit of good news deserves a fist pump even without an audience.

Thank the Lord for small favors. I decide I can give sleep another chance. Simply thinking about decorating the sorority house for graduation with Breanna in charge exhausts me. But like Martin reminded me, it will be the last grand decorating hurrah on the last lap of April's victory tour.

Chapter 4

I pick up three dozen assorted doughnuts on my drive to our sorority house. Hey, I'm all about making and keeping friends, plus I need something sweet to go with my coffee. This project will require lots of coffee.

Our sorority house was only a few years old when I moved in as a freshman pledge. It is still a source of immense pride for me, and I am grateful the present sisters continue taking loving care of the beautiful home. Recruiting and retaining quality members into our organization is difficult if the house looks like a wreck.

I open the front door and grin at the commotion inside the spacious foyer. Young women are scattered in small groups across the honey-hued pine flooring that doubles as our dance floor during parties. "Y'all started without me." I feign disappointment —poorly—because I'm sure my relief that they are out of bed shows clearly in my expression.

Breanna Coggins rushes to me. "It's just the last time you'll be here for us, April. Decorating has always been your thing, and we'll never be able to ask your advice again."

"I'm going to Atlanta, not dying. You can always call." I push the doughnuts into her hands. "In case the troops start to work too slowly and need a sugar rush."

Breanna's mouth forms an "O" and her eyelids hood. "Aww. You came to the rescue *and* brought treats."

"What's the status?"

Breanna points to the different groupings. "Rosemary and Amy are on the signage for the porch while Lisa and Maddie work on the crepe paper chains. Donna and Megan are helping Mrs. Brown finalize the appetizer menu, and Jessica, Sherry, and I are pulling out the graduation decorations."

I scan the room. Despite the girls' early start, they are just beginning to be productive. Worry lines crease Breanna's beautiful face. She sighs and twitches her neck, making her thick brunette ponytail, held tightly at the crown of her head with a vast red bow, swing like a pendulum as she waits for my comment.

"It sounds like you have a good handle on things. What would you like me to do?"

She exhales, and the stress appears to leave her body. Breanna sidles closer to me and gestures toward Lisa and Maddie. The girls sit at an eight-foot table. "They're not getting the crepe paper folds tight enough. It's looking more like a twist than an actual chain. Your chains were always perfect. Can you show them how?"

It is a shame I can't get paid for making crepe paper chains. I do make the best-looking ones in the world. "Sure, no trouble." I flip open the top of one of the doughnut boxes and grab a chocolate crueler.

I favor Breanna with a smile, bite into a treat, and sashay to the paper chain production table.

By lunchtime, we are making some serious progress. The first decorations are hung on the walls and railings like they have been for the previous six years.

Mrs. Brown enters with a platter of half sandwiches piled high and announces it is lunchtime. When she answers one of the girls that the tasty-looking sandwiches are chicken salad, my mouth begins to water.

My phone rings as I walk in a trance toward the powder-blue platter. I pull out my phone. *Martin.* If he were a lesser friend,

I would reject his call and pick up a sandwich—or two—instead. "Hey, make it quick. I'm kind of in the middle of something."

"She still hasn't called."

"Penny?" I shake my head as soon as I say it. How stupid. I have chicken salad on the brain.

"Yeah. What do you think is up?"

"It's not quite noon yet. Maybe she is sleeping in?"

Martin clicks his tongue. "She is like a rooster. You know she wakes up at the crack of dawn."

No. I didn't know. Now I have the weirdest visual of Penny walking around the bedroom crowing and scratching at the carpet with her bare feet. Thanks, Martin. It will take weeks for me to dump that out of my mind. "I wonder if her car is still there."

"Yeah. I've checked like four times. I couldn't sleep."

Okay, that isn't stalkerish at all.

"What do you think is going on?" he pleads.

I have nothing. Not a clue. That isn't entirely true. I have something on my mind. Still, telling my best friend I believe his girlfriend might be between the sheets with someone else is not a conversation I aspire to have.

"I've got to call the police."

"Martin! Don't call the police."

"I've got to report it, April."

I may punch Penny in the face the next time I see her. "Listen, let me finish up here, and we'll go to her house together. She might go easier on you for being a bonehead if I'm with you."

Martin's voice rises an octave. "Why would Penny go easier on me if you're with me?"

"Because she hates me. She will focus her anger on me. Not you." Man, I am so brilliant.

"She likes you. She likes you a lot."

My poor, sweet, delusional, love-struck friend. "Keep your word that you won't do anything until I get there."

"I didn't exactly agree that I wouldn't—"

"Promise me!"

"Okay, but hurry up."

I nearly bump into Breanna as I turn back toward my worktable. "Is everything all right?"

I nod my chin upward. "Yes, but I must help a friend out of a jam, so I need to leave in the next hour."

Breanna's eyebrows knit. "But you were talking to a guy."

"Uh-huh." I trump her with my own highly arched eyebrows and pointed glare.

Her face flushes red, and she looks away. "I'm sorry. I shouldn't have listened in."

True, but I don't feel like being petulant today. I *finally* reach for a chicken salad sandwich and let the eavesdropping incident drop.

"It's meant so much that you came to support us." Despite my feelings about Breanna, she will be an excellent president. She instinctively knows when to spread the compliments on thick. "You showing up to help today has been such a lifesaver."

"It's been my pleasure." As a former president, I know the political language and how to graciously accept her compliment.

I survey the progress as I quickly devour another chicken salad sandwich—half. "Where is the huge paper-mâché *Congratulations, Graduate* centerpiece?"

Breanna's eyes widen. "We couldn't find it. Do you know where it is?"

There are only so many places to hide a decoration that bulky. When I pledged our sorority, the house had a few vacant rooms. Over the years, the sorority's popularity has grown exponentially. Now, all but the senior girls share rooms. "It wasn't in the basement?"

Breanna's face screws up. "If it is, I couldn't see it for all the Halloween and Christmas decorations."

That is true. I remember now that last year I was concerned that if we put the graduation decoration down in the basement, we wouldn't be able to find it again. I asked the girls to put it in—bless it.

Of all the lousy luck. I guess I will not get off campus without saying goodbye to Rhonda Riley.

"It's in Rhonda Riley's old room," I say with a sigh.

Discomfort flashes across Breanna's face. "That decoration is getting a little tired anyway. We can do without it."

"Don't be silly. We dropped five hundred bucks on it three years ago."

Breanna shakes her head slowly. "Yeah. We'll just let it be."

Chicken. "I'll go get it."

"You will?" She looks shocked. "You are the best."

Whatever. I must get this over quickly to check on Martin before he does something stupid. I don't have time for Breanna's indecisiveness. "I'm gonna need a couple of girls to help me. It's awkward to carry."

"Lisa and Maddie, please go with April and help her get the graduation centerpiece."

The two girls rise from their paper chains and walk toward me without a clue. Of course, Breanna would send the freshman pledges who don't know any better. If they are lucky, they still won't know any better half an hour from now.

When someone is afraid of ghosts and you make fun of them and call them superstitious, you should understand something. Sometimes people aren't simple-minded. They are fearful of ghosts because they *see* ghosts.

And ghosts are really freaking creepy.

The girls follow me dutifully up the stairs toward the third floor. I try to normalize my breathing and tamp down the anxiety bubbling inside me as we walk up the stairs.

College is hard. Everybody wants to talk about partying and the great times, and there are many of those. Still, transitioning from childhood to adulthood and separating from your family unit is stressful. If you add the expectations of high grades at an accredited institution, mix in a social life that includes alcohol and occasional experimentation with illegal drugs, and top it off with the opportunity for sexual encounters with multiple willing partners—suffice it to say that it is a lot of moving parts for most students to handle.

Some folks handle it okay, others not so well, and then there are the Rhonda Rileys of the world. The ones who don't make it.

The ones who break your heart.

I was a sophomore when Rhonda pledged. She was pretty, intelligent, and came from a good family. We weren't super tight, but we could relate because both of us had struggled with our first major and blossomed in the business law program.

Rhonda was friendlier and more gracious than I am on days I'm at my best. All the girls loved her. None of us saw it coming.

I place my hand on the doorknob to her room and wait. If I had only paid attention to Nana Hirsch, I would have had enough control of my skills to scan Rhonda's room with my mind. Instead, I'm forced to hope I get lucky.

"What's the matter?" Maddie asks.

I conceal my hesitation with a smile. "Nothing."

That is what I feel: nothing. I hope it stays that way.

I open the door. Cautiously, I crane my head in and am greeted by a stale, musty scent. The room must have been closed up tight for months.

So far, so good. Thank goodness for small blessings.

I flip the lights on and push the door as far as its hinges allow. Tugging one of the many storage boxes toward me, I prop the door open with it. One of the few things I did pick up from Nana is to always keep your exits open.

The suite is one of the larger in the house. It was only available for Rhonda because it is on the third floor. Most of the sisters preferred to be on the first or second floors.

Despite the size, only a six-foot square area under the paddle fan in the center of the room remains clear of boxes. The room's balance holds tubs of varying sizes, four and five high and seven rows deep to the walls.

"It's not in one of these tubs." I direct the girls. "It's in a wooden crate about five feet long and three feet high."

"What is all this crap?"

I nearly laugh at Lisa's horrified expression. "Old records and retired keepsakes that people couldn't stand to throw away and stuff the girls who graduated decided not to take with them, that someone thought we might need later." I shuffle toward the center of the room. "AKA junk."

Lisa picks up a container and sets it on the one I used to prop the door. "I'm surprised they haven't had us in here cleaning this up." She puts her hands on her hips and scans the room. "I think I would really like this room."

Probably not. Unless she is one of the lucky few who doesn't even get goosebumps when there is a disturbance in the electromagnetic field that surrounds her body. "Yeah, it's not bad."

Maddie squeezes between a row of tubs. "It will go quicker if I climb up on top of these tubs and take a look."

"Bad idea. Many of the tubs are only partially full and would probably collapse."

Maddie huffs and resolves to get busy searching.

Ten minutes later, there is a growing stack in the center of the room and still no sign of the wooden crate with the centerpiece. The girls glisten with sweat. Their foreheads and cheeks are striped with smudge marks from the layers of dust on the tubs and boxes.

The lights of the old paddle fan in the center of the room blink in five short blips. I'm not surprised. The cold chill that evaporates the sweat at the back of my neck brings on a shiver.

"That was weird," Lisa remarks. "I wonder what caused that."

I don't need to wonder because I know. I continue to act nonchalant as I stack more tubs.

As I lift a discarded lamp from the top of one of the stacks, I spot the wooden crate four rows back against the wall. "Score."

"Did you find it?" Lisa asks.

"Y'all, I don't feel so good."

I turn to look at Maddie. She is directly under the fan. Her mouth hangs open, and her coloring has turned green. I ignore the ghostly scraped knees inches from her face. "Do you need to go sit down?"

Maddie swallows hard and grimaces as if she is about to hurl. "I don't know. I hope nothing was wrong with the chicken salad."

It has nothing to do with chicken salad. "Go to the restroom and put some water on your face. Maybe it will help."

Maddie stumbles out of the room. Lisa passes directly under the fan, yet it doesn't faze her. Lucky girl. I would give anything to be totally immune to spirits.

Lisa and I thump tubs around for another fifteen minutes to clear our way to the wooden crate. We attempt to lift it, but it is too heavy for us. So, we get behind it and push, sliding the container out of the room.

Once we have the crate in the hallway, I reenter the room to shut the door. Eyes to the floor, I slide the tub out of the way and reach for the light switch.

Don't look, April. Don't look.

Darn it. I'm going to look.

Rhonda's ghost remains precisely how I remember her the first time I saw her hanging from the fan. Her face is gunmetal blue, her head lists to the right, and her left ballet slipper hangs precariously on her foot.

It has a hypnotic quality to it. The longer I stare, the more mesmerized I become.

So many questions are left unanswered. They will remain unanswered forever. How does a seemingly well-adjusted girl, with friends and family who love her dearly, choose to end her life by hanging herself?

Her gashed knees just below the hem of her skirt always hold my morbid fascination. Did she fall on the way home to hang herself? How absurd does that sound?

The sadness washes over me like so many times before. I take a deep breath and exhale. "Goodbye, Rhonda. I hope you find peace," I whisper as I reach for the light switch.

Rhonda's eyes open, and I nearly pee myself. The scream I try to release emerges as a tiny squeak. I freeze in place.

Her eyes are milky white. No iris. No pupil.

The initial shock wears off, and I become mesmerized again. By the peculiar appearance of Rhonda's eyes, she has never opened them as a ghost before today.

She reaches out toward me with her left hand palm up, as if beckoning me to join her. The light switch flips off, and the door shuts so fast that I don't realize I did both until I have time to process the event while staring at the closed door in front of me.

As I squeeze the brass doorknob still in my grasp, I feel the thrum of her energy beyond the door. There is no denying it now.

Lisa watches me as if I am the most peculiar person she has ever known. "Are you okay?"

No. "Yes. But I'm running late, and I promised a friend I would meet him. Can you get some other girls to help you carry this down?"

"Sure, no problem."

I check in on Maddie, who is already looking better. Which I knew she would once she got out of the presence of Rhonda. I tell the rest of the girls goodbye and promise I will stop by Saturday after graduation to celebrate with them.

Rhonda remains on my mind the entire trip to Martin's apartment. I dig through my memories of her, trying to remember if she ever alluded to being depressed or mentioning taking her own life, even in jest.

I thought she had transitioned well to college life. The only momentary hiccup was when she, like me, switched her major from engineering.

Rhonda was destined to do remarkable things. She had even decided to earn her juris doctorate like me.

People with her level of ambition don't kill themselves. Right?

I don't know. The whole thing has seemed weird from the day I received the terrible news about her passing.

It might bother me less if I had been the one to find her and if I had seen her before they cut her down. But I hadn't. And yet her ghost appeared to me the first time I'd entered her room after she passed. When Tiffany Jones described the scene of how she found Rhonda, and every detail was the same as my vision—down to the slipper half kicked off and the scraped knees—it put a chill in my blood that I swear I feel to this day.

The ability to see spirits came to me through my maternal grandmother, Nana Hirsch. She is a self-proclaimed witch. I'm not sure if it's true, but she makes a convincing imposter if it isn't.

Other than my brother Dusty and me, Nana Hirsch is the only relative who claims to feel, hear, or occasionally see spirits. That isn't totally true. Granny Snow claims to see Jesus regularly, but that is an entirely different topic.

Before leaving for college, I never realized that seeing spirits was odd. Having other people in my family afflicted with the same "gift" made it commonplace in my small circle.

In the broader world of the University of Alabama, I realized just how rare it is to have an extra level of senses. Most of my friends don't get the slightest tingle on their necks when passing a restless ghost.

I am envious of their oblivion.

Soon I dropped all references of the supernatural sort outside my immediate family. Over time, pretending it wasn't a thing has dulled my spiritual senses. I eagerly buy into the theory that by continuing to ignore them, I will be what I desire most one day—normal.

Rhonda's ghost effortlessly tore a hole in the protective partitions I constructed around my mind. Her spirit is desperate in its struggle to be seen and acknowledged. It is precisely the opposite of what I would expect from someone who voluntarily punched their ticket off this plane of existence.

Her slipper has always been at that odd angle. It's funny how certain things stick in my mind for years on end. I mean, I'm standing there looking at a ghost. Hello! That should be horrifying and overwhelm every atom in my body. My friend's face is blue, her neck bent at an awkward angle. She is dead, and that is what should occupy my mind.

But it's not. It is Rhonda's scraped knees and that blasted slipper hanging precariously balanced on the end of her toes.

How does someone scrape their knees so deeply while hanging themselves that blood streams down their shins and congeals? If she were kicking her feet when she died, wouldn't her shoe remain on or fully fly off? How does it stay balanced on the tip of her big toe?

Bless it. I must get Rhonda out of my mind. If I hop back onto

29

that hamster wheel, my brain will burn out for days on end. I know this from experience.

Besides, done is done. Even if I could solve the mystery, it won't do Rhonda any good. It is best to leave the questions that haunt me in the past where they belong.

Chapter 5

I park in front of Martin's apartment complex and text him. He locks his door and takes the stairs two at a time on his way down to my car.

"I about gave up on you, Snow," he says as he buckles his seat belt.

"Sorry. I ran into an old friend that slowed me down." I pull out of the lot.

"I called her roommate, Monica, about an hour ago. I was hoping that Penny was with her. Maybe that was why her car was there, and maybe her phone died while they were out together."

A workable theory. Assuming Penny would bail on Martin to go out with her roommate without being kind enough to let Martin know and not ask to borrow her friend's working phone. There are a few too many *minor* logic flaws in Martin's theory for my taste. "I take it by your tone she wasn't with her."

"Nah. Monica was with some guy out on the Warrior River. She left before Penny went to the tutoring class yesterday."

"Quit being such a worrywart. Teaching those dummies all night must be exhausting. She probably decided to sleep in." It is a weak explanation, but it is the only one I can come up with at this point.

"It's one o'clock. Nobody sleeps until one o'clock in the afternoon. Not even rock stars and bartenders."

An excellent point. The tingling between my shoulder blades intensifies, corroborating Martin's assumption that something is amiss.

The little bungalow Penny and Monica share is on Azalea Avenue. As we take a right onto their street, I instantly note the revolving blue lights. My stomach rolls over, and the electric tingle shoots from my shoulder blades down my arms into my index fingers. This can't be good.

"Is that the police?" Martin asks.

It is, and plenty of them, so I assume his question to be rhetorical. Besides, they aren't exactly in front of Penny's house. Maybe it's her neighbors.

"Oh no!" Martin turns toward me, his eyes wild with fear. "April!"

My chest constricts. *Keep control, April. You've got to keep control.* "It could be anything, Martin. Don't be jumping to conclusions."

Three police cruisers idle on the road, the lights of another rotate in the driveway behind Penny's car, and an ambulance is backed up beside it with the rear door open. I pull in behind one of the cruisers across the street and throw my car in park.

"There's an ambulance. That's a good sign. Right?" Martin's eyes twitch wildly as he practically begs me to agree.

I don't know how they do it in Tuscaloosa, but Doc Crowder, the medical examiner in Guntersville, picks up his "patients" in an ambulance. The beacon lights of the ambulance in the driveway are off. I calculate the odds to be about sixty-forty, not in Penny's favor.

I unbuckle my seat belt. "Wait here. Let me go check it out."

"No!" Martin pushes his door open. "I need to know."

I start to argue but think better of it. If the roles were reversed, Martin wouldn't be able to stop me. Besides, if something terrible has happened, it isn't like I can protect my friend from the awful news forever.

I rush to grab his elbow for moral support. He is so intent on the police cars, I don't think he notices my hand.

"She is okay. I know she is well," Martin chants as we stumble toward the house.

We step over the curb onto the closely cropped crabgrass. A young female officer notices our approach. She lifts her hands, palms out, and intercepts us in the middle of the yard.

"What do you think you are doing?"

I increase my grip on Martin's elbow to steady him in case we receive unwelcome news. I purposefully lower the mental wall that prevents me from reading my friends and family's thoughts.

So sue me. I would be a fool not to use everything at my disposal at a time like this.

"That is my girlfriend's house."

The young officer's demeanor changes as her eyes narrow. A slight sheen of sweat glistens on her forehead. "What's your girlfriend's name?"

"Penny. Penny Trickett," Martin blurts.

The officer's lips tighten into a harsh, determined frown. She squeezes the button on her walkie-talkie. "Sergeant, can you come to the front yard?"

"Yes."

I feel Martin's confusion and concern turning to aggravation. "The least you can do is tell me if she is okay."

The officer's expression hardens, informing me Martin will not get any information from her. "Sir, you need to stay still until the sergeant gets here."

Martin pulls away from me, cutting to the right of the officer. "You can't stop me from checking on my girlfriend."

The officer takes one smooth step to her left, effectively blocking Martin. I suddenly realize she is an extraordinarily tall and athletic woman.

She arches her eyebrows and lowers her chin as she addresses Martin. "Sir, I'm going to tell you one more time. Stay right where you're at, or you'll wish you listened to my command."

I grab Martin by the arm again. Now I sense he is contemplating bull-rushing the officer. That would be a terrible decision. Martin might outweigh her by thirty pounds, but the officer looks fast and lethal.

"Martin! There is nothing you can do. If Penny is hurt, the EMTs are in there." I point toward the officer. "She has probably been instructed not to say anything. She called her sergeant. What more do you want?"

"Some answers!" Martin shouts.

I press my hands against his chest. "You're not helping anything. Just shut your mouth." He continues to glare at the officer, and I wave my hand in front of his face. "Down here."

His attention shifts to me. The intense despair emanating from his chest through my hands forces tears to my eyes. "I know it has to be tough not knowing, but let's stay calm until they have the situation under control."

He exhales, and his heart rate slows. He is almost calm. Suddenly he lets out a bloodcurdling scream of anguish as he pushes against my hands so hard he nearly bowls me over. I follow his line of sight just in time to see the sheet-covered stretcher lift into the back of the ambulance.

I clutch at his arm to regain my balance. His emotions crash into me with such force I fear my legs will buckle. I lean forward and wrap my arms around him in a bear hug for self-preservation.

"No!" he screams.

I hug his heaving chest as I struggle to keep my feet. Tears stream down my cheeks as his bare sorrow overwhelms me.

This is the worst. I can't believe this is happening.

And now I'm questioning my advice not to ring the doorbell last night when Penny didn't answer her phone. Had someone broken into her house? Was there a sign of a break-in? Was she still alive and needing help while Martin watched her home?

No to the first two questions. Martin would have noticed if her door had been busted. While he hadn't rang the doorbell, on my recommendation, he lurked outside her house half the night, waiting on any sign of her.

But what if he rang the doorbell like he wanted to do in the first place? *Stop it.* It isn't my fault. We wouldn't have automatically assumed she was in trouble if she didn't answer the door. We wouldn't have called the police either.

Would we? Yeah. Probably beat on her bedroom window first, but then we would have called the police.

I am restricting most of Martin's motion, but this doesn't prevent him from inching us toward the front door. The police officer appears uncomfortable with the raw emotion Martin is displaying. She backpedals toward the house, keeping us in front of her with her hand resting on her taser.

We are near the sidewalk as a middle-aged man who appears to use too many steroids steps before the officer. "Martin Culp?"

"Yes."

The sergeant pivots toward the officer who initially detained us. He favors her with a quick upward nod of his chin. "Go get her, please."

He turns his attention back to us. "I understand you called your girlfriend's roommate about an hour ago, expressing concern for her safety."

Martin pushes me to the side and faces the sergeant. The two of them take the measure of one another. "Yes."

"You mind telling me why you thought someone needed to check in on Ms. Trickett?"

"She was supposed to meet me last night at my apartment. She never showed up."

"And where were you?"

Martin hesitates briefly. "The first part of the evening, I was hanging out with April." He gestures toward me. "The rest of the time, I was at my apartment."

The sergeant's eyes shift from me to Martin and back to me. "Are you two dating, too?"

"Lord, no," I answer much too quickly. "We're just friends."

The sergeant pauses. When I don't add anything else, he takes a pad from his shirt pocket and holds a pen to paper with an expectant expression. "Mr. Culp, what is the name of your roommate?"

"I don't have a roommate."

The sergeant lifts his pen. "So, you have no alibi?"

"Why do I need an alibi?"

The sergeant flips his notebook closed and returns it to his pocket. "I can't comment on an ongoing investigation."

"Investigating what? What are you investigating?"

"You'll find out soon enough."

Martin takes a step toward the sergeant. "The other officer said you would answer my questions."

The sergeant locks Martin with a deadly stare. "I guess that makes two of us disappointed our questions aren't getting answered."

"What does that mean?" Martin yells.

"That's him. That's the boy I saw."

The tall, athletic officer leads a small, elderly woman toward us. Her hair is a blue-gray halo of curls around her weathered face. Her eyes open wider as she points her long, shriveled index finger at Martin.

The sergeant observes her with great interest as the female officer asks, "You are sure, Ms. Gates? The dark makes it hard to see anything besides silhouettes."

Ms. Gates jabs her pointy finger in Martin's direction. "Oh, that's him. I will never forget that face. On several occasions, passing vehicles lit his face up perfectly. The dark doesn't bother my eyes a bit. I've got the eyes of a twenty-year-old. Just ask my optometrist."

I don't need to be psychic to understand the direction of this discussion. It triggers all my senses to be on high alert. "Martin checked to see if his girlfriend's vehicle was in her driveway. We hadn't heard from her all day and were concerned for her safety."

"Then you were with him?" The sergeant's eyes bore into me.

No, I was the idiot telling him to come by and look. The sergeant's steely expression convinces me not to test a white lie. "No, sir, I wasn't."

The sergeant favors me with a "bug off" glare. "Then what do you have to do with this conversation?"

I stare at him blankly. He is right—all my legal training tells me that—yet it seems so different since it is personal today.

"I was just checking to make sure that nothing happened to her car and that she made it home safely," Martin says.

"Then you admit to being here last night?"

I grab hold of Martin's wrist as my training belatedly engages. "Sergeant, we need a few minutes before Mr. Culp answers anything else. He is in shock from the loss, and given that you have failed to read him his Miranda rights, it wouldn't matter much anyway."

I tug on Martin's wrist hard and lead him forty yards from the sergeant's harsh gaze.

"What does all this mean, April?"

"Martin, these guys think you hurt Penny."

The color drains from his face. "Why in the world would they think that?"

Honestly? "You had the opportunity—Ms. Gates saw you walking around. And you had a motive—Penny stood you up. Plus, you notified a friend to check on her, and now you are at the crime scene."

He gestures toward the ambulance. "The sheet. They might have pulled it up to keep the sun out of her eyes. Right? I mean, it is bright today."

This Band-Aid is going to hurt coming off. "Martin, I think Penny may be dead."

It occurs to me that Martin might push past me and make a break for the ambulance. I also think he might scream and collapse into a fit of sobs. I do not anticipate him to pass out and fall straight backward. He barely clears the base of an oak tree before his head bounces off the ground twice.

Chapter 6

They take Martin to the local emergency room to treat him for a concussion. After that, they transfer him to the county jail. I have the unfortunate honor of contacting his parents and explaining the situation.

I choose to leave out that I was the friend who convinced him not to check on Penny the night before for fear that she might be cheating on him. It is a struggle, as my guilty conscience wants to come clean.

The only positive I can find is that with Martin in jail, I have no distractions to keep me from preparing my apartment for my family's arrival tomorrow. It is an excellent time to borrow my landlady's vacuum cleaner. I routinely vacuum my carpet quarterly, whether it needs it or not.

After vacuuming, I buy cabinet polish, oven cleaner, and toilet bowl bleach at the supermarket. I even remember to purchase a toilet brush.

Six o'clock p.m. rolls around quickly. I sit at my three-chair kitchen dinette set and inspect my abode with a discerning eye. *Darn, girl. You ought to clean more often.*

My apartment is immaculate. It wasn't this clean when I moved in.

I realize I haven't eaten all day and resolve to take a quick shower and see what I can hunt down on fast food row.

The lights of the city blur into a kaleidoscope. The tears welling in my eyes have much to do with my current vision impairment.

Martin's predicament has knocked the shine off the week for me. It should be an exciting time for both of us—graduation and heading off to our dream jobs. Instead, he is in jail, and I'm driving around aimlessly, unable to decide what I want to eat for dinner.

Life can really bite at times.

In the morning, I wake up with what feels like a hangover. My headache seems unduly unfair since I didn't drink a drop of alcohol last night. I stagger to the kitchen and make coffee. The earthy aroma calms my nerves. I slump at my dinette with my mug cradled between my hands.

This can't stand. I understand why the police are so ready to charge Martin. Lord knows if I hadn't been with Martin the day before and known first-hand how much he worships Penny, I would arrest him, too.

But he is innocent. I know that for a fact, but the police don't. Since Martin has no alibi, there is no need to investigate further. The police believe they have their man.

I must get off my butt and help Martin. I might not just be his best chance of proving his innocence; I might be his only chance for freedom.

My nerves falter as I drive back to Penny's house. I began to hope that her roommate or the police would be present, so I could use that as an excuse.

Ignoring my psychic skills had been a conscious decision on my part. Just like muscles, the power atrophied, but it never entirely disappeared. What can I say other than "once a freak, always a freak."

Ignoring my skill has allowed me to be "normal" most of the time during my college tenure. But there are rare occasions when I wish I understood how to use my skills to their full extent. Those times when I wished I could marshal the entirety of the power I think of as "extra juice." I'm not feeling it today. I doubt I will be able to glean the information I need from Penny's house. Still, I owe it to Martin to try.

Keeping with the Randy Leath tradition, I park a block down from the crime scene. I walk by her house once to check for police cars on either side of the road or her roommate Monica's car in the driveway. When I confirm Penny's home is empty, I continue to the end of the street, make a U-turn at the stop sign, and come back as if I am a power walker out for her Friday morning hustle.

When I approach her mailbox, I stride casually onto the driveway, walk to the privacy fence, and enter through the gate. I pause there to catch my breath since I stopped breathing several yards back. My adrenaline has spiked hard, and I feel a light sheen of sweat under my shirt.

This is incredibly stupid. I don't have the skills for private investigation. I think to leave, spin around in a circle, and change my mind thrice quickly. Nice. Now I look like a dog chasing her tail.

I must get a hold of myself. Martin would do this for me.

That is true. But I know Martin is a better friend than I am.

To overcome my nerves, I make a deal with myself. I'll quickly check the back door and the four back windows. If they are all locked, I wasn't meant to enter Penny's house. Never mind that it would be nothing to break out one of the windowpanes in the back door and reach through to undo the lock.

Once on the back porch, I grab the doorknob. I'm confident I will find it locked. The door pops open without me even twisting my wrist.

Darn it!

Trained or untrained, I feel violence disrupting the air as I step into the family room via the back door. No voices, no visions. But the dark energy of violence is fresh.

That is the only residual energy left. I hoped for more—a vision of what had taken place. Preferably a point of view revealing who had been with Penny last night. That is what I had hoped for.

I'm not ready to give up yet. I center all my thoughts on Penny, pull the latent energy in the room into my sternum, and compress it into a tight ball within my core. I push the collected power outward with a rush, seeking any other residual powers.

After a few seconds of firing out my energy, there is still nothing.

Fine. I'll investigate the rest of Penny's house. As with Rhonda Riley, the locale is essential. If Penny met her untimely end in her bedroom, the energy imprint of her struggle would be there. I notice a hallway toward the front of the house and creep forward. The movement of a shadow at the half-opened blinds catches my eye. Instinctively, I duck behind the partition wall between the hallway and living area.

Then I carefully peep around the edge. The shadow remains on the front porch and is now stationary. My breath catches as someone cups their hands against the picture window, and the shadow leans forward as if to peer into the house.

I lean back behind the dividing wall and struggle to normalize my breathing. Police? No, they would have a key.

No matter how hard I try, I can't force my mind from racing to the obvious. Criminals like to return to the scene of their crime. Penny's murderer could be standing on the front porch basking in his sick glory. The thought of it chills my blood.

My survival instinct insists that I keep my back plastered to the wall and wait thirty minutes before moving. But my curiosity wants to know who is on the porch.

Curiosity wins out.

I slink along the wall until I'm a foot from the slatted blinds. I surmise that if he had to cup his hands, the sun's glare is in my favor. Craning my neck, I lean forward for a quick look, hoping my theory about the sun is correct.

It is a man—tall with curly brown hair with a significant amount of gray streaking through it. I can't see his face as he walks to his car. He opens the door to his convertible and slides in. As his profile comes into view, I choke. "Dr. Rosenstein?"

I'm relieved he didn't see me. I would've felt foolish if he found me in Penny's house. There is nothing like one of your professors finding you skulking around inside a murder victim's home.

But what is Rosenstein doing on the porch anyway? Did he know Penny or her roommate? I can't recall Martin ever mentioning Penny having a class with Rosenstein. Then again, I might have let it slip my mind.

I continue my examination of the house. In each room, I try to reach out for any residual energy. Like in the living area, there are trace levels of violence, but that is all I receive. Overall, it is a bust. But at least I can say I tried.

My phone rings, and I nearly jump out of my skin. I look down at caller ID and grin. "What up, bro?"

"My appetite. Where are you? Your front door is locked."

Like all the men in my family, my brother Chase is easygoing and kind. His flat stomach belies the enormous number of calories required to keep him happy each day. He is perpetually hungry.

"I can be there in about twenty minutes."

"Dude, I'm starving."

"I'm sorry. I'll be there as soon as I can. Where do you want to go?" I speed walk toward the back door.

"Hey, Dusty. You want Baby Ray's?" Chase asks. "Really? OK." Chase speaks into the receiver. "The rib connoisseur has selected Wonderland Ribs."

Excellent choice. Zero atmosphere and great ribs. "You want me to just meet you there?"

"Yeah. That is a great idea."

Chapter 7

My brothers are exceptionally tight. They're supposed to be; they're twins. Fraternal twins, to be exact. You would be hard-pressed to identify them as brothers if you met them. They look nothing alike.

Dusty resembles a gigantic teddy bear. Standing at six foot five inches and weighing over three hundred and twenty pounds, he is a considerable-sized man. His hair is red and exceptionally curly. His skin burns at the first hint of sunlight.

Dusty is also filthy rich. After graduating from Auburn—the enemy college—with a Ph.D. in physics, he has earned a small fortune as a nonfiction ghost story writer. A fortune his ex-wife works overtime to purloin from him in divorce court.

My other brother, Chase, makes Hollywood's favorite heartthrob actors of the month look plain. He is six foot two with perpetually bronzed skin, panther-like muscles, and an easy smile with lots of white teeth.

He is also a player.

Chase plays at hunting, fishing, water skiing, golf, and darts. You get the picture. He also rebuilds and re-finishes cars in his spare time when he isn't running the family marina. He took over the daily activities of the marina rather than go to college.

I know that Chase hasn't had a girlfriend in years. He dated Barbara Elliott throughout high school, and the entire family assumed they would marry after graduation. Something happened toward the end of their senior year that ended their relationship. Neither Chase nor Barbara ever talks about what happened.

I pull into the gravel parking lot of Wonderland Barbeque. I'm not usually squeamish. Still, I am glad Rodrick finally built a privacy fence behind the small, flat building. It serves as a blind so the customers can't see the pigs in the muddy yard behind the restaurant.

Some people like to pick out their lobsters from a tank, but watching a pig while eating pork is a little much for me.

It is still a little early for lunch, and my brothers are the only ones seated in the restaurant. Chase's back is to me. Dusty waves and stands as I enter. He starts toward me, laughing as he clomps heavily across the worn wooden floor. He is sporting an unkempt red goatee that juts outward from his chin. "There's our new lawyer."

"I have to finish the bar first," I remind him.

He picks me up and squashes the air out of me. "Just a walk in the park for you."

I don't have the breath to respond. I'm thankful that Dusty puts me down and starts patting my shoulders.

Dusty's smile fades. "You look different. Are you okay?"

Chase leans in and hugs me, too. "Dude, she is getting old. Don't draw attention to it. Women are sensitive about that."

I pop Chase in the chest with my fist. "I'm tired. Not old."

Chase shrugs. "I don't know. You're close to the witching hour. Can women even have babies after thirty?"

"Thank you for the concern, Chase. I love you too."

Chase is tickled that he baited me successfully and chuckles as he gestures toward the table.

I narrow my eyes. "And for the record, I just turned twenty-six."

"He knows. He is just jerking your chain," Dusty says as we take our seats.

My two brothers are inseparable. Even their different lifestyles and mutually busy schedules don't prevent them from spending all their downtime together.

Despite our age and gender difference, they always allowed me to tag along. Dusty and Chase have never made me feel like the third wheel I'm sure I am. I am blessed to have such wonderful brothers who have encouraged me to be fearless and do my own thing while standing ready to do triage if I screw up.

I didn't realize until now how desperately I have missed them these past few months.

"Where are Mama and Daddy?"

"Dad had a report to file at Redstone this afternoon before he could leave," Dusty says.

Chase flashes his dimples and white teeth in a grin. "Then he has to go pick up Nana."

"Nana is coming?" That is a bit of a surprise.

Dusty raises his eyebrows. "Granny, too."

"In the same car?"

Both brothers laugh.

"That is gonna be like geriatric WWE."

"I got a twenty on Nana." Chase mimes as if pulling his billfold out.

"I wouldn't rule Granny out. You need to watch out for those mild-mannered little ones. Sometimes they are cold-blooded killers," Dusty says with a surprisingly straight face.

My brothers and I have a lot of love for both our grandmothers. There is no love *between* our grandmothers. Granny Snow is a Bible-thumping President Reagan conservative who lives on a ranch. Nana Hirsch is a bona fide pagan witch who worked on all of George Wallace's and both of President Obama's campaigns. The two women believe each other is the Antichrist. I consider them to be oddly more alike than different.

"There's going to be some serious fireworks in that backseat," I predict. "Will Dad survive it?"

Dusty shrugs. "I'm sure they both realize that it's not about them. They are both immensely proud of your graduation."

That is sweet for him to say. But it is a bit too idyllic to believe that the two women will put their differences aside for five minutes, much less a day.

"So, what else is new?" Dusty asks.

That is a loaded question. My brothers have met Martin, but I'm not sure they will remember him. "Do y'all remember my friend Martin?"

Dusty shakes his head, and Chase points at him. "You know, the tall, red-headed dude. He looks like that prince that just got married. What's his name?"

"Prince Harry? I offer.

Dusty nods his head. "Oh yeah. I remember him. Wasn't he getting a law degree, too?"

"Yes. Martin has been in most of my classes."

The left side of Chase's lips tug upward. "You two little devils aren't getting it on, are you?"

My face contorts into a grimace. "No! Lord, no."

My brothers share a look and break into toothy grins.

"I think she doth protest too much," Dusty remarks.

"Are you going to let me tell you my news, or do you plan to just keep talking nonsense?" I huff.

"I can aggravate you all day long and never get bored," Chase claims.

That is a true statement, as teasing me to the point of torment is Chase's special gift. I direct my attention to Dusty. "My *friend*, Martin, his girlfriend…"

"Wait. So, you're not his girlfriend?"

I roll my eyes as I turn back to Chase. "How many times do I have to tell you we're only friends? We had this same conversation the last time I mentioned him."

"Yeah, but I was thinking friends with benefits."

"Absolutely not. Just friends."

Chase frowns. "Now that's highly disappointing. Here, all this time, I thought you were hooking up with somebody you liked."

I know better than to let Chase get under my skin. But it is akin to ignoring a flea in your sleeping bag. "Like you've been dating anybody in like, what, the last, I don't know, decade?"

"That didn't bother me because I was living vicariously through you. But if you don't have anybody special—I don't know. Now I'm feeling kind of empty and sad."

"You're kidding, right?" Dusty interrupts.

Chase hollows his cheeks and blinks his eyes as if fighting off tears. "No, man. That means we're all three losers. When I thought April was hooking up, I felt like I had a prayer of meeting somebody. I'm doomed now."

"If you're doomed, it has nothing to do with April."

"Excuse me, I was trying to tell you something important." Once I have their attention, I fill in the rest of the current dilemma. "Martin's girlfriend was found dead this morning. The police took him into custody for questioning."

Chase scratches his chin. "Was she, like, murdered?"

"Of course, she was murdered," Dusty volleys back at Chase.

"I didn't know. She might've had a heart attack or been a diabetic or something."

"Hello, why would they take Martin in for questioning if she died of a heart attack?" Dusty asks.

Chase begins to answer, pauses, and then laughs. "Dude, I guess you're right."

"I don't know what to do to help him. His parents are coming in tonight to bail him out, but this is going to put a damper on his graduation tomorrow."

"April, you know how these things go. There is an eighty-nine point six percent chance that Martin killed his girlfriend. That is an indisputable fact." Dusty shrugs his meaty shoulders. "Your friend is going to have more to worry about than his graduation being awkward. He will need to worry more about the forty years he'll have to serve and who his bunkmate will be."

My idiot savant and run-of-the-mill idiot brothers are beginning to drive me nuts. "Martin is innocent, Dusty."

Dusty takes a moment to study my face. Whatever he is searching for, he doesn't seem to find it. "How do you know?"

"Mostly because I was on the phone with him the majority of the night."

Dusty's brow creases. "April, that doesn't prove anything, and it certainly wouldn't hold up in court."

I glare at him. "I know that he is innocent."

"Just playing the devil's advocate here, but couldn't he have called you right before he killed her and right after?"

"Dude, that is so cold," Chase says.

"Can I help you?"

I look up at our waitress. Tall with an athletic figure, her hair is straightened and frames her dark face. Her black eyes are large and presently locked on my brother Chase.

"Hi there." Chase makes a show of looking at her name tag. His gaze lingers on the small fabric opening just below the top button of her blouse. "Teresa, my brother tells me that the ribs here are the best in Tuscaloosa, so we probably need to start with at least two racks."

"You can't go wrong with the ribs. What else can I get you?"

"I sorta like surprises. I'm up to trying everything you like, Teresa."

Teresa stops writing on her pad, grins and rolls her eyes. "I don't think you could hang through all of my favorites."

Dusty bursts into a booming laugh. I'm forced to bite my lip, so I don't tell Chase to quit while he is behind.

To his credit, Chase continues to smile and doesn't miss a beat. "It would be fun to find out for sure."

"Uh-huh." Teresa scribbles a couple more things and asks what we want to drink.

After taking our drink orders, she saunters off to the kitchen. I don't like to doubt my brothers, but Teresa is right. Chase wouldn't be able to hang with her.

"Do you even hear yourself?" Dusty asks.

"What? What did I say?"

Dusty ignores Chase as he locks eyes with me. "Sounds like your friend Martin could use a well-trained clairvoyant. Somebody who could go to the crime scene and sense what happened."

Dusty has always been less than understanding that I don't want to develop any of my many psychic abilities. He has minor skills, but my talents are easily ten times more powerful.

"I already went to the murder scene. There is hardly any residual energy in the house. I felt some violence in the aura but zero female energy."

"You did go to the murder scene?" Dusty leans forward.

"Martin's my friend. Of course, I tried."

Dusty shakes his head slowly. "With it being the scene of the murder, it doesn't make sense that there isn't any residual. Violent deaths almost always leave an emotional signature. Assuming the spirit doesn't remain on this side of the veil."

Chase picks up the sweetened tea Teresa set in front of him. "Unless it's not."

"What's not?" Dusty asks.

"Not the murder scene." Chase takes a sip of his tea and smacks his lips. "Just the way I like it. A little tea in my sugar."

"But her roommate found her there," I insist.

Chase exhales. "But it might not have been where she was killed. Everything might have been staged to look like that is where the murder took place." He waves his hand. "You guys know all this spiritual mumbo-jumbo better than I do. But I'm guessing if Penny was murdered somewhere else, the energy you keep talking about would be there. Not at her house."

Chase might not be a Rhodes scholar, but his command of basic logic sometimes puts scientists to shame. "That's right. That does make sense," I say.

Dusty squints. "Maybe so, but that doesn't help your friend in the least."

"No. But I was assuming that I didn't have enough juice. It's more likely that it took place somewhere else."

"I don't mean to argue, but since you never trained your talent, there is no way you would know for sure. I mean, you spent the last seven years trying to bury it, April."

"It works just fine, Dusty."

"You can't know that."

"I found Jaxx, didn't I?" I remind my brother how I was instrumental in finding a kidnapped child earlier in the year.

"Yeah, and you acted like it was an odd series of dreams, not some form of psychometry."

The stress over the past few days bubbles over. "I know it works, okay? It never quit working. Yes, you're right. I have been trying to ignore it for the last seven years. No matter how much I try, it keeps coming back. I know darn well that it's working because I encountered Rhonda Riley's ghost less than twenty-four hours before I checked Penny's house."

Chase cocks his head at an angle. "Who is Rhonda Riley?"

Dusty opens his eyes wider. "Did you say ghost?"

Did I say ghost aloud? "Host. Rhonda Riley, the host."

Chase screws up his face. "Host of what?"

Dusty eyes me suspiciously. "No, you said ghost. You wouldn't be holding out on me, would you?"

Oh my gosh. I can't win with these two. I have never been allowed to have secrets. "Darn, Dusty. It's not like I work for you."

"It's not like I haven't made it clear that I'll pay you a thousand dollars for any verifiable leads."

I flip my left hand over and favor him my best 'are you kidding me?' look. "You think a thousand dollars is worth becoming a social outcast in my sorority?"

"She is the hostess at your sorority?"

"Quiet, Chase!" Dusty and I yell in unison.

"Tell me about the ghost." Dusty clasps his hands while he stares at me unblinkingly.

"Why did I think you two might help me clear Martin's name?"

"Because three heads are better than one. Tell me about the ghost, and I'll help you with Martin. Is it a partial? Please tell me it's a partial."

Oh, what the heck. Dusty will pester me to death until I tell him. We have time to kill before the rest of our family arrives anyway. "A full female apparition."

Dusty exhales so comically loudly that it makes accidentally spilling the beans about Rhonda almost worth it. "No way."

"I've got no reason to lie," I remind him.

"Have you tried to record it?" Dusty asks.

Why would I want to do that? "No. I'd be happier if it just went away."

"But a complete apparition?" Dusty shakes his head. "Wow."

"I haven't seen anything this complete since the Freeman plantation." I throw that comment in before thinking.

Dusty's excitement melts as his face turns white. The Freeman plantation is where Dusty's paranormal career started. On a lark, as teenagers, we slipped into the condemned, decrepit plantation renowned as a paranormal hotspot. I came face to face with my first full apparition as a reward.

Everything had been going to plan—as much as possible when you're hunting supernatural entities—but when the apparition started making like Stretch Armstrong by stretching his arms toward Dusty, let's just say it wasn't an orderly retreat. Our quick exodus was complicated when Dusty fell through the rotten stairs on our way out the front door.

"Has the apparition shown any violent tendencies?" Dusty asks in a lower voice.

"Nothing. Of course, I don't hang around to see if it changes its mind."

"Huh. A ghost without an agenda. That's refreshing," Chase comments.

"There is always something," Dusty argues.

Teresa placed our ribs, mac and cheese, fried okra, pinto beans, and chowchow on the table. I'm wrong. Chase can hang through all her favorites.

At the end of the meal, Teresa reappears, clears our plates, and slides the bill in front of Chase. Chase snatches it up as Teresa walks away.

"I've got this," Chase declares as he eases out of his chair.

"Wait a minute," Dusty growls. "Let me see that tab." He holds out a meaty, expectant hand.

"No, really, my treat."

Dusty gestures a come-hither motion with his fingers. "Give it here."

Chase sulks and then slaps the paper into Dusty's hand.

Glaring at Chase and holding the tab in the air, Dusty asks, "How do you do this?"

Teresa had penned her name on the handwritten ticket, followed by a local phone number.

Chase grins. "What can I say? I just have a magnetic personality."

Chapter 8

Since we have more than a few hours to kill, I decide to take my brothers over to the sorority house. It will be a win for all three of us. Dusty will get to see a ghost—assuming his skills are up to the task. I can make a quick thousand dollars since I have already opened my big mouth about Rhonda Riley. And Chase will be able to check a life goal off his bucket list of visiting the inside of a sorority.

The girls have done a fabulous job on the decorations. Of course, there is room for improvement, but they won't embarrass themselves without my assistance in the future. That is bittersweet.

I introduce my brothers to the girls we meet as I lead them to the third floor. What greets me in front of Rhonda's closed bedroom door gives me pause.

Ghostly energy surges and shimmers around the doorframe. As I lightly press my fingers to the doorknob, a tingling sensation works its way up my palm and collects in my wrists.

Something is up, and it unsettles my nerves. The back of my neck tingles like a multitude of spiders scrambling from my hairline and down my spine.

"Dusty, be ready. There seems to be a higher level of energy now." I glance at Chase. "You might want to hang out here."

Chase scans the empty hallway. "But nothing is happening out here."

Chase has never sensed a ghost, much less seen one. But I'm not in the mood to argue with him. I've done my part by warning him. "Suit yourself, but don't blame me if you get possessed."

I open the bedroom door, and the same stale, musty scents greet me. Still, the ghostly glimmer around the doorway, portending a surge of magical energy, is not present inside the room.

Surveying the room's disarray from the earlier search for the missing decoration, I consider asking my brothers to help me organize the jumbled containers.

Nah. I'll leave that for the girls to clean up. Besides, Dusty's experience with hauntings is more valuable than his brawn. With any luck, he may be able to clear Rhonda's spirit from the room. That would benefit my sorority sisters more than re-stacking some boxes.

"Is it here?" Dusty asks. "I can't sense or see anything."

"If she makes an appearance, she'll appear at the..." I point my finger toward the ceiling fan in the center of the room. My finger curls back toward my palm as Rhonda materializes in her now-so-familiar macabre pose.

"What is it, April?"

"Shhh."

"Did you just shush me?" Dusty asks.

"She is here—now."

"Where?"

When Rhonda Riley appeared to me for the last five years, she did so as a full apparition. But until today, because full-body ghosts are extraordinarily rare, I had not realized she was always in a semi-transparent state. If I didn't know Rhonda died five years ago, the clarity of her features, coloring, and clothing would have me believe I am looking at a person, not a ghost.

Gingerly, I step closer to her. The wound on Rhonda's knee oozes a shiny sheen of blood. Her hands are the most surprising shade of violet. Her face is dark gunmetal gray with an angry raspberry-red abrasion just below the climber's rope cinched around her neck. Her silver ballet slipper still hangs at the precariously odd angle. Just a whisper of breath would knock it from her toe.

Emotions flood over me. It is a mixture of profound grief for the loss of life and awe of the supernatural spectacle I see, coupled with guilt for not understanding Rhonda's need for support. Maybe I could have convinced her life was worth living if I had only known. I squeeze the back of my neck to chase the tingles away and return to the present.

"She is right in front of you, Dusty."

His head twitches side to side. "I don't see anything."

Dusty's inability to see a ghost isn't that unusual. He might be pulling down half a million a year authoring supernatural tell-all books. Still, his ghost-sighting talents are minuscule and random. He can most days sense spirits, sort of a goosebumps meter when one appears close to him, but whether he sees it or not is a haphazard proposition. It is a cruel irony of life that I have a much more comprehensive and substantial skill. I don't want my "gift," but Dusty could make wonderful use of the talent, as it would benefit his chosen career significantly.

"I'm with Dusty." Chase has his hands in his back pockets and still manages to shrug. "I don't see anything but a bunch of boxes."

I allow for the randomness of Dusty's spiritual sight and play to his strengths. Sliding to the left of Rhonda, I gesture for him to step forward.

He favors me a sideways expression of doubt that says he isn't a hundred percent convinced but walks toward the fan. I motion for him to stop as he nears Rhonda, but his belly taps her foot.

I watch, mesmerized, as the silver slipper swings forward, back twists to the left, and falls to the floor. My blood chills as I stare at the dark leather bottom of the slipper lying on the dusty pine flooring.

"Uh… I think I feel something. Something cold."

My mind races. What have I just witnessed? I stare at the sole of the ghostly ballet slipper between Dusty's boots and Rhonda's purple big toe pressing against his belly.

"Dude. Do these girls always keep it this cold in the house?" Chase opens his mouth and blows. A small puff of white fog billows from his lips. "Holy crap."

Not good. Rhonda's ghost has never been this active. My limited experience with active apparitions is they tend to wake up in a foul mood.

"I wish I could see her." Dusty stretches out his left hand.

"Don't do that." I panic as Dusty's hand presses against Rhonda's waist.

"It's like I can feel her. Her energy. It's different than the rest of the air."

The uneasy feeling in me increases. "If you can't see the ghost, let's leave."

"I want to take some pictures first. Something might show up."

"Hey, guys?" I swivel to Chase's voice. His face, no smiles now, has a green hue. "I don't feel too good. I'm going to stand outside." The sense of impending doom is so overwhelming I don't remind Chase that is where I suggested he stay all along. I begin to leave with Chase, then notice movement in my periphery.

First, Rhonda's fingers stretch like she is waking from a long nap. Rhonda raises her arm slowly, as I have seen a few times in past visits.

"You need to take a few steps backward, Dusty, or you're going to get the brain freeze of a lifetime," I warn.

His goofy grin clues me in that he has no idea what I am talking about. Still, he dutifully backpedals just in time for Rhonda's hand to clear where his chest had been seconds earlier.

Rhonda's hand extends upward in that peculiar motion I have seen on many occasions. But I am relieved. All the times before, I assumed she was pointing at me. My active guilt had me believe she was either implicating me for my failure as a friend or trying to convince me to follow her to the plane where she now resides. Now that she is pointing in Dusty's direction, my long-held belief evaporates.

"Move to your right."

Dusty's voice rises an octave. "You're not leading me into the arms of an angry ghost, are you?"

"You need to work on your trust issues." I gesture for him to hurry. "You should know I don't want to be the one to explain to Mama and Daddy how you got abducted and eaten by a rogue spirit."

He lurches to the right with a halting laugh. "I can't believe you would waste a talent like yours."

Rhonda's accusing finger sweeps slowly to the left of Dusty. "I wouldn't expect you to understand. You like being different. I want to be normal."

The movement of Rhonda's hand stops abruptly, and her index finger appears to double in length, unnaturally, causing me to shudder as the creepiness repulses me.

"You really should—"

"Hush for a moment," I hiss.

Rhonda's finger continues to elongate now to the length of a ruler. I freeze with my jaw hanging slack. I wonder when it will stop growing.

Her head snaps to the right, and her milky-white eyes flash open.

The heel of my shoe slaps into a box as I reel backward. My hands windmill to keep my balance, finally recovering and saving myself from a nasty spill into the filthy boxes.

I stare at the thick layer of dust I had almost tumbled onto and draw a breath of relief. Reluctantly, I continue to follow the direction of Rhonda's outstretched finger.

A grouping of five pictures printed on copier paper secured to the wall with yellowing tape seems to appear out of nowhere. I turn and move closer to the collection on the wall.

There is a picture of Rhonda and the nine other girls who pledged our house her freshman year. Clustered around it are pictures of her at her first tailgate party, the homecoming float, a girl's night at one of the local bars, and a group photo from one of the infamous Chattahoochee River excursions.

Have these always been here? Did the girls and I uncover the pictures when moving the boxes?

"Am I close to touching her?" Dusty asks in an exaggerated whisper.

I blink rapidly. Dusty's hand plunges through Rhonda's midsection. "You should be feeling something about now."

"You know, I swear I do."

I slip between boxes and tubs to the recently exposed printouts and lean in for a closer inspection. I am in three photos with Rhonda from her freshman pledge year. We look so young, so happy.

The photo of the rafting trip that Professor Rosenstein hosts every year is a little more complicated to identify the members. The student groups participating in that event are a true cross-section of the campus and far more eclectic. Professor Rosenstein is mindful to invite a mixture of Greek and non-Greek, female and male participants. I manage, with some effort, to identify all but two in that year's rafting trip.

Seeing all the familiar faces in the other photos brings a smile to my lips. I welcome it, given the sadness which permeates the room with Rhonda's ghost on permanent, grisly display.

"Do you think she would show up in photos?" Dusty whispers.

I blow out an exasperated breath. "I don't know. I haven't exactly researched it. That's your deal." I don't mean for it to come out so harshly, but the idea of photographing her seems, well, exploitative.

"Who will I need to talk with to get permission to research the house? I would like to bring the team here soon."

"Breanna Coggins is the president of the house. You'll want to discuss it with her and the housemother."

Chase pokes his head back into the room. He is an even darker shade of green. "Hey, can we go?"

I step toward the doorway and point down the hall. "The bathroom is the fifth door on the left, Chase."

Chase's face changes to shock. "Isn't that, like, a girl's bathroom?"

"It's not gender-specific. Besides, it has a lock on the door."

"Yeah, I'm good. I don't want to throw up in the girl's bathroom."

"Hey, Sherlock, Robin is about to hurl, and he'll only do it at my apartment. Why don't you come on so I can lock up?" I direct toward Dusty.

Dusty's serious face dissolves into amusement. "I think you have your characters jumbled together."

"Whatever," I say.

I feel vaguely better about Rhonda when Dusty drives us to my apartment. She has been hanging dead in that room for so long, and even if it is only in my mind, it is as if she never lived life.

But she did.

The printed pictures on her wall are a testament to her life. I cannot know what sort of woman she would have become. Still, in the brief time she was at the University of Alabama, she left an indelible mark that her friends will remember forever.

Chapter 9

Mama's white Suburban occupied two parking spaces outside my apartment. She is not a terrible driver. Her car is just that big and the parking spaces that small.

"Will miracles never cease?" Chase points to the SUV.

"I figured the next time I saw that car, it would be a burned-out husk because Nana and Granny had gotten into a battle in the backseat," Dusty adds.

The boys are privy to some history I have never witnessed. I am aware, albeit secondhand, that the two women do not agree on anything. Given their disparate religions, it doesn't come as a complete surprise.

I open my apartment front door to find Daddy on the opposite side of the kitchen table dressed smartly in a navy-blue suit with a striped tie. None of the women in my family are in view.

"There is my smart girl." Daddy closes the space between us and gives me a fierce hug. "Are you excited?"

"I've got enough butterflies to fly me to San Diego if I could tie a thread around their legs."

"Let me go check in my luggage. I might have a spool of butterfly thread."

We both laugh at the old joke that connects us. Even if only by the thinnest strand of butterfly thread.

I look over his shoulder. "Where are Mama and my

grandmothers?"

Daddy rolls his eyes. "Your mama is reading them the riot act out back."

"Seems like you should be involved with that, being Granny is your momma."

"There is not a single woman out there who listens to me."

That is the truth of it. There is no need for me to agree with the obvious. "I hope y'all already ate. The boys and I went to Wonderland."

"Not yet."

"When were you planning on going to dinner?" I feel awful that we didn't call to check if they would like something to eat before we left the restaurant.

"I wish I could tell you. I'm just along for the ride."

Typical Daddy. If he and his brother Howard have any faults, it is that they are often too easygoing.

"No one else from Guntersville is coming for the party?" I ask.

Daddy points to some gifts on my kitchen table. "Your uncle wanted to, but he has a prior engagement. He sent a gift and told me to tell you he loves you and is proud of you."

"I was hoping to see him. I don't know if I'm going to be able to swing by Guntersville when I leave for Atlanta next week."

Daddy's face twists. "Why not? It's on the way."

"No, it's not, Dad. Atlanta is to the southeast. Guntersville is northeast of Tuscaloosa. She would be adding at least four hours to her drive." Chase knows his way around the interstate system.

"You're not going to come home? Not even for a couple of months?" Daddy's large, maize-colored eyes implore me through his thick glasses.

I didn't made a single trip home during the last seven years where someone didn't complain that I wasn't returning to Guntersville after graduation. Heck, as far as I am concerned, the reason I went to college is so I *don't* have to go back to Guntersville.

Do parents believe they can change their children's minds if they ask their children something enough? Why will they not accept my adult decisions? It irritates me to no end that my parents still think of me as a little girl who needs their directives.

"Daddy, we've gone over this at least a hundred times. Occasionally, I'll come home to visit, but there are many more opportunities in a major market. I can't limit myself and end up like Uncle Howard with a tiny law office just off Guntersville Square."

"Your uncle does a fine business." Daddy's cheeks flush red. The brothers' loyalty runs deep.

"And that is great for Uncle Howard. I'm happy for him. But I want something different. Something more profound."

Daddy uses one of his favorite lines again.

"Big-city living isn't all it's cracked up to be."

"And it may not be. But I want to learn firsthand, not rely on someone else's opinion."

Dusty encircles us with his arms. "You shouldn't have coddled her so much when she was little. Now you raised an elitist."

My blood pressure surges up as my body flushes with angry heat. "I'm not an elitist."

Dusty smirks. "All right. Whatever you want to say."

I turn to Chase for support. "Chase, tell them I'm not an elitist."

Chase wrinkles his nose as he walks toward the refrigerator. "I'm not even sure what an elitist is. Do you have any beer?"

"You do know what an elitist is," I mumble. "There is no beer, but some pinot noir is on the bottom shelf."

Chase pulls up short of the refrigerator and shudders as his face draws up in disgust. "I'm good."

The sliding glass door bangs open on its track, drawing all our eyes. Mama, taller than most women with willowy legs and arms, stomps into the room. Her thick, chestnut hair is pulled up into a makeshift bun—messy yet elegant—and her jaw is clenched tightly as she rolls her vibrant brown eyes. "Those two are impossible."

She gives me a quick squeeze and a kiss on my forehead. "It's so good to see you, baby. I'm proud of you."

"Thank you, Mama."

"Can you hurry it up? I'm practically melting out here in this heat," Nana complains to Granny's back.

"Hold your horses, Pauline."

Mama closes her eyes and shakes her head. "Lord help me. I'm going to put up the cutlery to be on the safe side."

The two women who amble through the glass door look about as different as their personalities. The taller woman with olive-colored skin and thick, shoulder-length pewter-gray hair has angular facial features, intense dark eyes, and high cheekbones. Even in her seventies, Nana is an impressive woman.

In front of her is Mrs. Claus. Or at least her white hair, creamy porcelain skin, round face, deep-set blue eyes, and short yet plentiful physique allows Granny to be an uncanny double for Mrs. Claus.

A definitive aura of brightness surrounds both women. The illumination originates from the powerful gifts they were blessed with at birth.

Tolerance for one another's religion is not one of their gifts.

Granny hugs me and holds onto my left hand. "You get prettier every year, April. You favor your great-grandmother Snow so much."

"Nonsense, she looks like a light-haired, light-eyed version of her mama." Nana bumps Granny away as she comes in for a hug and places a peck on my cheek. "I'm so excited you'll be able to visit next week."

Oh my gosh. "Nana, I start work next week in Atlanta. You—"

The front doorbell rings.

"Were you expecting someone?" Daddy asks as he takes a step toward the door.

"No, sir. I'll get it." My roommate Julia is supposed to be spending the night with her boyfriend. I can't imagine who it could be.

Two dark-suited men fill the small landing of my front porch. "April Snow?" the thinner of the two men asks.

"Yes?"

"I'm Detective Green, and this is Detective Cunningham from the Tuscaloosa southern precinct. We were wondering if you might have a moment to answer a few questions."

I have a sinking feeling in my gut that promises to remain with me for the rest of the evening. "I would be glad to." I make to pull the door closed in hopes of talking to the detectives outside, but the door's motion comes to an abrupt stop.

"April, what's up?"

I look over my shoulder and continue tugging the door behind me. "Nothing, Daddy."

"Gentlemen, what is this about?" Daddy asks.

"Nothing that concerns you, sir," the larger of the two men says to my father.

"That is my *daughter*, so it *does* concern me."

First, it is embarrassing for the police to show up at my front door when I have company. Made even more incredibly awkward when that company is my family. But it might be a wee bit more embarrassing when my daddy puffs up his dad-bod chest and acts like he plans to pick a fight with a detective. A detective with a freakishly large physique who appears more than willing to squash Daddy with one hammer fist to the head before body slamming him to the floor and zip tying his wrists behind his back.

The giant detective favors Daddy a grin that looks like a wolf licking its lips.

"Daddy, I've got this." I'm compelled to push him back across the threshold as I yank the door shut. I return my attention to the detectives. "Sorry about that. Do you know if Martin posted bail?"

The two men eye each other before the thinner of the two speaks. "I don't think Mr. Culp will be able to make bail."

I attempt to keep the shocked expression off my face. "Yes, he will. His parents are coming up from Texas."

"Just because your mommy and daddy show up doesn't mean you get set free on the world. Especially if you're a murderer." The giant detective, who could have played offensive tackle for Alabama sometime during the last decade, sneers at me.

"Martin is not a murderer."

"Well, going on that premise, I am hoping you can help us with the timeline of events last night."

My arms instinctively cross my chest. This conversation isn't going to be positive. "Sure, if it will help Martin, I will do anything."

"Yeah. That is what we're afraid of."

I am unsure why Detective "Bigs" has a problem with me, but my patience has worn thin. "Excuse me, did I do something wrong?"

"I'm not sure. That's why we're here talking to you."

The thin detective shoots the giant man a glare that wipes the snarl off his face. At least now I know who is running this circus.

"It really won't take long, Ms. Snow. We prefer to go over these details at the precinct if you don't mind."

I snort a most unladylike laugh. The last thing I need is to sit for a couple of hours answering questions at the police station.

Why don't they use some of the highly sophisticated DNA machines my professors have raved about over the last three years to tell them who did what? If they don't believe Martin, I don't know how interrogating me will improve their belief in his honesty.

"I'd rather not."

"I'm sure Ms. Trickett would rather not be dead, too," Detective Cunningham snipes.

"It's not that I'm not willing to help. It's just that you guys have terrible timing. My entire family is visiting to celebrate my graduation. I can't just hop up and leave them."

"I assure you it will only take a few minutes," Detective Green tries to assure me. "Again, all we wish to do is establish the timeline."

Refusing to be helpful isn't in my blood. Besides, the thinner gentleman, Detective Green, seems levelheaded and honest enough. I decide it best to follow them to the precinct and answer their questions.

"Let me get my keys."

"No need. We can run you down to the station and have you back before you know it," Detective Green coaxes.

I am not thrilled about the prospect of relying on these men to bring me back to my apartment. But I suppose that if I wish for the police to trust what I say about Martin, it might be helpful if I reciprocate a little trust in their direction.

I reopen the front door and holler to my parents that I will return shortly. I conveniently omit the details about the cops wishing to ask me questions at the precinct. They're not stupid. They'll figure it out on their own.

Chapter 10

Going for a ride in the back of an unmarked police car is not on my "things to do" list on the evening before graduating from law school. I have been expecting to spend time with my family before I leave for Atlanta, and this excursion is seriously eating into my celebration time.

In all fairness, Martin had planned to spend quality time with his family, too. He isn't merely inconvenienced by a couple of questions. Martin remains in police custody, enjoying a tiny room with a seating choice of a cot or a stainless-steel commode.

I have no idea what happened to Penny. But I do not believe Martin is capable of doing anything illegal. Bless it, Martin would have found Penny hours earlier if I hadn't convinced him not to pound on her door when she didn't respond to all of his calls and texts.

Even as I replay through my head the details of the night Penny died, I still am unsure what course of action Martin and I should have taken. It seems like one of those impossible situations where any action I could have chosen would have been incorrect, and Penny would still be dead.

The detectives lead me into a room slightly off the front counter of the precinct. Detective Green motions for me to sit.

"Would you like water or a Coke?"

"Not right now. But thank you for asking." I sit, and Detective

Green does the same. Cunningham appears content to lean his massive frame against the wall and glower in my direction. I suppose he is concerned any standard chair would simply buckle under his weight.

"Ms. Snow, how long have you known Martin Culp?"

"Three years."

"Would you say Martin Culp has been a good friend during that time?"

"I consider him my best friend."

Green scribbles something down in his notebook. "Do you two share secrets?"

Secrets? "If you mean do we talk, yes."

"Do you two talk about things you don't talk to other people about."

"I suppose both of us had times that we told the other something and never told anybody else, if that is what you're getting at."

Green shakes his head. "I'm not getting at anything, Ms. Snow. I'm simply asking straightforward questions and would expect direct answers in return."

And here I thought I might like Detective Green. "Just for the record, your direct question sounds a lot like a leading question."

Cunningham shoves off the wall. "And your answers sound evasive."

Oh, he has not seen evasive yet. I favor Cunningham with my best "burst into flames and die a painful death" stare.

"Ms. Snow, please understand. We want to help your friend, too," Detective Green continues.

"Really? Because back at my apartment, it sounded like y'all are convinced that he is going away for life."

"I'm not going to understate the importance of getting to the truth. Penny Trickett deserves justice."

My eyebrows jump into my hairline. "Justice? How about justice for an innocent man? And let me remind you that every minute you spend trying to put Martin in jail is more time for Penny's killer to make a getaway."

"Why are you so sure that Culp is innocent? Has he promised you something in return?" Cunningham questions.

Boy, Cunningham is such a lovely man. "I'm convinced because I was either with him or on the phone with him most of the night. In the three years I have known Martin, he has never shown even a hint of a violent temper. Has he promised me something in return? Not exactly, but I would anticipate a continuation of our friendship."

Green slumps in his chair and sighs. "I can appreciate your loyalty to your friend. You need to know that witnesses can establish an opportunity for your friend. Of course, the motive is indisputable."

I can't help but laugh. "The motive that he was madly in love with her?"

Green's eyes narrow. Cunningham tilts his head as he stares at me as if I have lost my mind.

"What?" I ask with an exaggerated head shake.

"Penny Trickett was three months pregnant. That could be a motive to get rid of her if she wanted to keep the baby and Mr. Culp didn't."

I gasp for air. Penny... pregnant? Why wouldn't Martin have mentioned that?

Still, Green's conspiracy theory rings hollow.

"If Penny were pregnant, Martin would have been ecstatic. If you didn't hear me the first three times, he is graduating with a law degree tomorrow. That is if you guys don't jack it up by falsely hanging a felony around his neck. He will be a high earner and would be ecstatic to share it with Penny and their baby," I insist.

"Unless the child was somebody else's." Cunningham folds his massive arms across his chest.

"Do you two hear yourselves?" I wave my finger wildly in the air. "You don't even know Penny, and you are putting her in bed with multiple men like she is some harlot. Degrading the victim to hang a crime around the most convenient suspect seems like pretty lazy police work."

Both men's expressions harden. Good, I have struck a nerve. I won't be winning the Miss Congeniality award after all. Boohoo.

The room remains uncomfortably silent. Green is drawing random circles and triangles on his legal pad. Never trust a doodler. Their minds are never at rest.

"So, you admit that you were with Mr. Culp most of the evening. Correct?"

Green is back to his leading questions. "Yes."

"We have many witnesses telling us that you two are close. Extremely close."

I scoff. "Bless it. I told you we are best friends. Aren't best friends supposed to be close?"

"Some of these witnesses say you are more than best friends—intimate." Unfortunately, Cunningham rejoins the conversation.

"Lord, no."

Green continues, "These witnesses state you and Culp are in a relationship. That would certainly be more complicated with Penny still around."

I stand. "Listen. I did my part. I told you everything I know about that night. I have been forthright with the information about my relationship with Martin. I explained that he was in love with Penny. If I were to guess, he is devastated. Martin is probably worried about Penny and her family, when he should be worrying about how he will defend himself against detectives who want to hang the murder of his girlfriend on him just so they are not late to dinner."

I slide my chair under the table.

"Where do you think you're going?" Green asks.

"I'm leaving. I have visitors at my place. If you plan to charge me with anything, you would already have done it."

Cunningham sidesteps in front of the door, effectively blocking my progress. He places his ham-sized hands on his hips and widens his stance to bar the entire exit.

"You might want to move, Detective Cunningham. Otherwise, you are going to be singing soprano in the choir for the next few years."

Cunningham reluctantly steps to the side of the door. He looks like he would love to rip my head off. I have no doubt he could manage that task with relative ease.

I stick my tongue out as I pass by him. It isn't mature, but it makes me feel better. I love living on the edge.

The door closes behind me, the adrenaline leaves my body, and the severity of the situation crushes in on me. The police are working an angle that may also pull me into Penny's murderer. This revelation bumps up the urgency of doing the detectives' job and finding the actual killer.

My mouth is dry, so I walk up the hall until I find a water fountain. As I lean over and take a sip, I hear a familiar voice. Professor Rosenstein is coming down the hallway, escorted by a female detective.

My body tenses as I remember the weirdness of Rosenstein peering into Penny's window the day after her murder. I can't explain it. It is one of those psychic senses screaming at me to pay attention. Without any further thought, I slip into one of the doorways in hopes that Rosenstein won't see me as he passes.

"I'll never understand evil people," Rosenstein declares to the female detective.

"That is why we appreciate leads like yours from the community, Dr. Rosenstein. Without those leads, we would never be able to take killers off the street and bring closure to victims' families. Justice can't be served without the public's help."

"Yes. Justice. It's not as good as bringing her back, but Penny deserves justice."

Penny? What relevant details could Rosenstein know about Penny's death? That doesn't make any sense to me.

I saw him at Penny's front door. Maybe he came back later and found something I failed to notice? No. The police stripped the property of anything that might remotely be considered a clue. When I explored her house, searching for energy imprints, there was nothing of interest.

Watching Rosenstein exit the building, my stomach cramps. The foundation of my life shifts.

It suddenly dawns on me that I effectively nullified the

promised ride home when I left the interrogation room. I take my phone out of my back pocket and tap Dusty's phone number.

"Hey, is everything okay?"

"No. The police are dead set on charging Martin with murder, and they are considering me as an accomplice," I say through clenched teeth.

"What? April, we might need to get Uncle Howard up here. Or maybe his friend, the district attorney."

"No, not yet." I lean my butt against the wall.

"I sure am sorry. This should be a joyous time for you and Martin."

"You know what would make it a little better?" I ask.

"Ice cream?" Dusty teases.

"That sounds good, but a ride home would be even better. Otherwise, I'm stuck asking the jerk detectives for a ride."

Dusty laughs. "That would be an awkward ride."

I join in with a laugh of my own. "Ya think?"

Chapter 11

I peer out the glass door while I wait for Dusty. The idea that the detectives are considering charging me as an accomplice scares me. Deep down, I have no doubt they would never be able to convict me, but juries are unpredictable at best.

Even so, just the charges would play havoc with my new position at Master, Lloyd, and Johnson in Atlanta. Lawyers are stripped of their bar accreditation when convicted of a felony. New hires can lose their opportunity with a firm over simple charges. There may be due process in the legal system, but not necessarily in the Human Resources department.

The air smells stale inside the police precinct, so I step outside. The thick, humid late-spring air envelops me.

Bile rises in my throat, and my equilibrium goes off kilter. From my past experiences, I begin to panic. *No, no, no.* I draw in short, measured breaths as I attempt to hold a migraine headache at bay. Despite my efforts, I know its arrival is imminent.

Migraine headaches have been the bane of my existence since my eighth birthday. Many are slightly more painful than an ordinary headache that I have trained myself to soldier through with a couple of acetaminophens or a handful of aspirin.

Then there is the "insert an ice pick at the base of my skull repeatedly while bright lights flash in front of my eyes" variety. The first symptom of this variety is typically nausea. I have a prescription for these debilitating migraines, but I don't carry the medicine with me since they are rare.

I lean against one of the brick columns outside the police precinct to stabilize myself. Only a few minutes have passed since I called Dusty. That fact does not stop me from scanning the horizon in hopes that I will see my brother's car coming into view.

The colors of the grass, trees, highway, and cars intensify. I close my eyes against the vivid stimuli. With my eyes shut, the volume of the environment around me increases until the din is deafening. The helicopter's close approach forces my eyes open, but only for me to realize the noise is merely a dragonfly passing in front of me.

Sweat trickles down my spine, as well as behind my ears. These, too, are tell-tale indications of the impending attack. I fumble my way down the brick column, taking a seat on the rough concrete. I pull my knees tightly against my chest and wrap my arms around my legs. "Please. Please."

The first electric-like jab at the base of my skull forces me to buck from the pain. The first jolt is always the worst. I can never fully prepare myself for the excruciating pain.

Once the first wave clears, I know I will be doubling over in pain every five seconds with the same blinding agony until the migraine subsides.

The second jab strikes, and I hear myself whimper. A blinding white light at the back of my eyelids accompanies the second assault. The taste of copper fills my mouth as my nausea escalates and the odd streams of sweat continue to pour from my scalp.

Leaning over, I hope to quell my sickness before it embarrasses me. Could the police arrest me for getting sick on their stairs?

My mouth waters profusely, and my stomach roils as if on fire. I pray I will vomit. At least I wouldn't have to fight the raging sickness in my gut any longer.

The subsequent pain tears through my skull. I am sure my head will explode from the pressure any moment now. Listing to the left, I barely raise my hand in time to stop my face from striking the concrete. The rough, sun-beaten texture of the pavement warms my palms.

Darkness rapidly envelops me. No sound, taste, or light exists for me as the world becomes void of all stimuli.

In the distance, I hear my little boy calling out to me. "Mama. Mama!" I smile, or at least I feel like I do. He lightens my heart as only a son can fill a mama's heart. Deep love and joy overwhelm me.

My joy turns, in quick succession, to confusion. When did I have a son? I can't remember. Oh Lord, what is his name? I have forgotten my son's name.

Bright light creeps back into the world. My body slides left, then right. Something squeezes me tightly, and I want to open my eyes. I think I can, but they are too heavy. Whatever holds me threatens to crush the air out of me.

"Mama! Come quickly. I need your help."

My boy, whom I can't remember, needs my help. I force my eyes open.

Dang. My son is massive. How old am I?

"What's the matter with her, Dusty?" another male voice shouts too loudly.

"I found her like this in front of the police station."

Something cold and soft tucks under me, and then not-my-son appears close to my face. "April, can you hear me?"

"Dude, why didn't you take her to the emergency room?"

"It's not like that. It's one of those stupid episodes April gets. She was talking in a different language again."

"I'll go find Mama."

"April, where is your medicine?"

What medicine? I wonder. Then a blinding pain emanating from the base of my skull forces me to curl into the fetal position as I mew in pain. The pain feels familiar, but not in a good way. The darkness approaches again, and I accept it willingly without question.

Female voices chatter around me. I open my eyes. I'm sitting in my bed, propped up by pillows. My brothers, Mama, and Daddy are lined up against the wall close to my desk. The expressions on their faces have me thinking that I might have been worse off than I feel.

How do I feel? Tired—but thankfully, the nausea is gone. Right. I'm aware I have suffered another one of my horrific migraine attacks.

A smoking bundle of sage waves in front of my face. I have always liked the smell of sage.

I follow the hand to its owner and find Nana chanting. This is a little disconcerting, although I'm not sure why.

I attempt to raise my right hand, but something holds it down—something heavy in my palm. And it is…

A sizeable crucifix. Granny kneels beside my bed, trapping my fist around the cross while she chants. Latin, maybe? It sounds vaguely familiar.

She looks up, and our eyes lock. "Pauline, she is awake."

"Vivian, hand me that potion. Please."

Mama comes into view at the foot of my bed. She holds a small flask.

Granny stands as she continues to speak in Latin. Yes, Latin. I have never heard those exact words, but they sound vaguely familiar.

Granny dips her finger into a cosmetic compact she holds in her hand, leans over, and draws a cross on my forehead. The Catholic-based action is most unusual, considering Granny is a Progressive Primitive Baptist.

"April, I need you to drink this. It will help you sleep. You need some rest for tomorrow." Nana uncorks the potion and holds the emerald-green bottle in front of me. Her hand slips behind my shoulders, and she lifts me into an upright position.

I want to ask her what is in the potion. I love Nana, but

sometimes her concoctions have disastrous side effects, which is when they work as she intended.

I flinch as the bottle approaches my lips. It is for a good reason. It is all I can manage not to jerk away as the glutinous, bitter, reeking concoction rolls across my tongue. This must be a joke. There is no way something that tastes so putrid could be healthy.

As she pulls the empty bottle away from my mouth, I violently shake my head. "What the heck, Nana?"

"Sorry. Some of the best medicine is the most bitter," Nana apologizes.

"A little warning next time?"

She peers over her shoulder at Mama. "See, Viv, it's already working."

Nana looks across me. "Anything?"

Granny pushes her hand to the small of her back and stretches. "Nope. False alarm."

I am groggy, but as ever, my curiosity is piqued. "What do you mean, 'false alarm'?"

"Don't trouble yourself about it, dear. You need to get some sleep," Granny says as she pats my hand.

"You know I won't sleep until I know what you're talking about. Spill it, Granny."

Her lips narrow as she stares at me disapprovingly. But she knows I am right. "You were speaking in tongues when Dusty carried you inside."

I try to process this, which isn't easy given my woozy state. I did learn a little bit of Latin as a matter of course in law school, and I know a few words of Spanish, though my pronunciation is pathetic. "Like Latin or Spanish?"

Granny offers me a quick shrug. "It was Greek to me."

I wish to discuss the matter more thoroughly, but my head feels incredibly dense. A warm, satiated state courses through my body. I have no choice but to push deeper into the pillows. The last thing I remember is the smile on Nana's face.

Sleep potions are different from sleeping pills. When sleeping pills don't work, you stay awake. If the creator doesn't mix a sleeping potion correctly, you will appear asleep but suffer from paralysis and be aware of everything around you.

Initially, I think Nana has mixed the potion incorrectly. Despite the darkness that surrounds me, my mind is fully engaged. At least as much as I can be in total blackness with no sound or smells.

It's an odd feeling being wired yet having no stimuli. It is mildly relaxing and a good bit scary. The fear comes from the knowledge that if the vacuum of stimulation continues, I will go crazy in a few days.

The relaxation is a blessing. My body has been in full stress mode for the last forty-eight hours.

More importantly, there is still something itching in my mind that I know I must remember. But with the constant turmoil of Martin's imprisonment, Penny's death, and my family's arrival, I can't focus long enough to identify what I need to recall.

There is a sudden, perceptible shift. One moment I am recounting my troubles from the day as I drift off to sleep. Then everything is blank for a beat before a new scene bursts to life in vivid color.

A man is straddling my chest, his large hands squeezing my neck.

I know it is only a dream, but the pain and burning in my lungs feel all too real. I claw at the man's face, and he pulls back just enough to prevent me from gouging his eyes. He slides his knees up until he has pinned both of my elbows to the ground.

Desperate, I thrash side to side to no avail. The only thing free is my legs. I knee him in the back as violently as possible, hoping to dislodge my attacker's hands from my neck long enough to gasp down a breath of air and continue the fight.

I have no effect as I attempt to kick my attacker in the back. He merely leans forward, his chin above my eyes. One of my shoes flies from my foot as I try to change the angle and kick my attacker again.

Over the urgency, the pain, and the fear, I become mesmerized by what I see. Resting precariously on the right shoulder of my attacker is a silver slipper. I had chosen it carefully that morning since it perfectly matched the silver in my blouse.

My life ebbs from me. I have no energy left to fight. As my body relaxes, the darkness returns, and I accept it greedily to escape the pain and violence.

Sadness overwhelms me as I realize what I have dreamt. Is it prophetic or a shared dream? After seeing Rhonda Riley twice in one day, it isn't far-fetched to think I would have a nightmare about her. Nothing confirms it as a true vision.

There is another lurch in the dark, signaling my dream state continues against my will. I fight it with everything I have, wanting desperately to wake up. I don't care to have to think about any of this.

Another too-bright scene replaces the darkness. I stand in front of Dr. Rosenstein. Unlike his usual happy self, he appears angry. His face is flushed red, and veins protrude at his temples.

"Absolutely not. You need to quit living in this fantasy world you have created," Rosenstein growls.

"You need to step up and be a man." My mouth moves, and I hear the words, but I don't know where the words originate from.

Rosenstein smirks. "You're right. I shouldn't complain. I should just take care of the situation."

"It's about time you came to your senses."

"Let's have a drink and talk about this like rational adults," he continues.

I place my hands on my hips. "Have you been listening to anything I've said? I'm pregnant, you fool. I can't have a drink."

Rosenstein waves his hand. "I meant juice or water, whatever you prefer."

"Do you have a diet soda?" Good Lord. Who am I? I would rather drink another one of Nana's potions than a diet soda.

"I believe so." Rosenstein holds up a finger, signaling for me to wait. He disappears through a doorway and raises his voice as he continues the conversation. "You know I didn't ask for any of this. You came to me."

I want to run. I already know how this story ends, and I need to get out of this house. *Now.* My feet remain planted as I glare in the direction of his voice.

"You weren't complaining about the deal when we made it. Besides, you got the better end of it. All you had to do was post a stupid grade for me."

"But now it's more. Now you need money for a baby I didn't ask for. Why don't you simply marry that chump boyfriend of yours?"

"As if. You couldn't pay me enough to marry either of you losers."

"Unless the payment was an 'A' in a class." Rosenstein appears with two sodas.

"You are such a monumental jerk. I should have just studied for the grade."

Rosenstein raises his eyebrows. "Finally, something we both can agree on." He hands me the drink in his right hand. "Let us discuss terms. If I am going to pay for a little brat, I expect visitation rights."

"No. Not happening," the body I occupy responds.

Rosenstein takes a sip, watching me intently over the top of his glass. "That hardly seems fair, and after all the quality time we spent together?"

"Screw fair. You pay in full and pay on time, or I report you to the dean. I'm sure he will love to hear about what you do with your students." I lift my glass to my lips.

No! Don't do it! Don't drink the soda!

The cold rim of the glass presses against my lip. I have no power to stop the motion. Semi-sweet liquid rushes across my tongue as it relieves my parched throat seconds before the effervescent bubbles tickle my nose.

Rosenstein smiles. "You've overplayed your leverage."

"Like heck I have."

I know Rosenstein is correct. Penny, the body I occupy, has cornered him, and when cornered, a killer's gonna kill.

I—*she* staggers to the right and only remains upright by catching hold of the sofa arm. "What have you done to me, Paul?"

"Eliminated you. Were you delusional enough to think I would tuck my tail between my legs and give you everything you want? How pathetic."

I lose the battle to keep my balance and fall forward, my face and swollen belly bouncing against the hardwood floor. My mind rages inside my paralyzed body.

A shoe shoves harshly under my chest, and I roll onto my back. Rosenstein's face appears, blocking out everything else in the world. "How did you really think this would end, Penny? You are a smart girl. Think about it, and you will understand that you didn't leave me any options. Eliminating you is the only logical plan of action left to me."

I attempt to scream and roll over. It is all in vain as my body is rigid, as if cast in concrete.

"There are so many sweet and torturous things I would like to do to you right now." A greasy smile envelops his face. "Oh, I would love to have the time to try them all. But it's just a matter of minutes before your loser boyfriend comes sniffing around your house."

He leans forward, kisses me on the lips, and then shakes his head. "Such a waste." He stands and disappears from my view.

For a few brief seconds, I forgot I already know how the story ends. I dare to hope he will be gone long enough for the narcotics from my soda to subside so I can escape. My panic grows in earnest as he straddles my chest and snaps a nylon climber's rope taut between his fists while baring his teeth.

Rosenstein dangles the frayed end of the rope over my nose and slowly strokes the brush-like fibers across my face in short, swiping motions. The ever-increasing fear manifests inside my paralyzed body.

Rosenstein leans forward, pressing his forehead to mine. "I'm afraid you will not enjoy this much, Penny. But I will."

His warm breath leaves a sheen of moisture on my face. All color begins to leach from my vision. I struggle to free my arms so I can claw at the rope biting into my neck. I cannot, and darkness fills my view.

This dark is different than the earlier version. I smell rich, aromatic coffee, the tang of hickory smoked bacon, the sweetness of Poison perfume, and fragrant, smoldering sage. My mind reaches obligingly to the familiar stimuli. The welcoming smells signal my escape from Rosenstein and the horror of his cruelties.

I struggle to open my eyes. If I can wake up, the bad dreams will be banished and I can search for meaning in the two horrific visions.

As much as I yearn to wake, something tethers me to the darkness, trapping me in this semi-conscious dream state.

I still have not remembered that critical item I need to solve the puzzle. My dread rushes to a frenzied state. What if I never wake up again?

"April."

I know that voice. I strain against the darkness, eager to end this trial.

"Come on, April. Wake up."

There is nothing like routinized behavior to break a trance. How many years of Mama having to wake me up in time for school has ingrained my now natural response when she tells me to wake up with that specific tone of voice. Obediently, my eyelids pop open, and the room's light forces me to squint.

"There you are. We were worried about you."

Mama sits on the bed with her hand on my shoulder. Both grandmothers still flank my bed—their faces are further creased with lines as they regard me carefully.

"What time is it?"

"It's five in the morning," Mama says as she feels my forehead. "How are you feeling?"

"Better. Now that I'm awake." I glance at Nana Hirsch, "I think you might want to dial back the strength on that one and put a warning label on it."

"Shhh." Mama rolls her eyes at me. "I don't think anybody else would have the same reaction as you, baby."

The double-feature nightmare has left me disoriented and angry. But Mama is right. The visions might have manifested —potion or no potion—once I went to sleep. Nana's bitter concoction facilitated rest, not necessarily the nightmares.

Nana moves further up the side of the bed until she is just behind Mama. "Did you have some sort of vision, April?"

I don't want to talk about it. I can't talk about it since it is too horrific. I look my Nana in the eye and lie. It is a good one because I don't even crack my usual goofy grin as I say it. "No, ma'am."

Nana's face draws in as if she has bitten into something particularly sour. "Oh."

"You don't have to talk about it right now." Granny bends forward and pats my hand. "But when you are ready, we are here to listen."

I turn my head to Granny's voice. Her piercing blue gaze bores into me. Her expression tells me she doesn't believe me. As she likes to say, I am full of baloney. But she is giving me space.

Nana taps Mama on the shoulder and gestures toward my bedroom door.

Mama pats my arm one more time as she rises from my bed. "If you're hungry, your daddy is finishing up on breakfast right now."

My deceitfulness shames me as I watch the women in my life retreat from my room. But it is too much to deal with all at once. A few days ago, I had little to worry about. A couple of finals that I knew I would ace, my dirty apartment to clean, and my walk through the graduation line were all that concerned me. Simple enough.

Now my best friend is facing life in prison, I might lose my dream job if charged as an accomplice, and the worst thing by far —my "gift" has begun to strengthen and grow. I can no longer keep it from appearing in unwanted cameos in my life right when my stress level is maxed out.

I have spent the last twenty years constructing a sturdy partition in my mind to keep me sane. The first fissures in the wall started during a trip to Guntersville that included an unfortunate boat accident. Then a month later, they reappeared during a friend's wedding. Honestly, it was a near-miss wedding. I put the kibosh on that celebration when I accused the groom of planning to off the bride.

I managed to do the right thing when using my "gift" that weekend. I might have saved my friend's life. But now, I am terrified I have woken the supernatural beast that resides in me. It will not rest until the wall that separates it from my sanity permanently falls, allowing it free rein over my life.

The thought of dealing with that level of weirdness on a daily basis terrifies me. I want no part of it.

This weekend is not anything I could have expected. I penciled this date in seven years earlier as the day for the most epic celebration in Tuscaloosa's history. Instead, it is one long, angst-ridden roller coaster ride, and I can't be sure the tracks aren't missing up ahead. I am one piece of unwelcome news away from a complete meltdown.

I bounce the heel of my palm off my forehead. There is still something I must remember. It is like taking a test and knowing you studied the answer, then drawing a complete blank when the time comes.

It has something to do with Martin. Or at least his case. I wonder if it would be possible to visit him. Maybe if I could talk with Martin, that all-important recollection would surface.

I loathe the idea of going back to the police precinct. My shoulders shake involuntarily as I recall how indignant and scared I felt in the interrogation room. I hate how they insinuate I did something wrong, and I especially don't care for how isolated I felt in the room with the two detectives.

I wish Martin didn't have to go through this alone. I have enough natural meanness to fake toughness when I'm in a horrible spot. But Martin? Martin is way too sweet. The fact that the girl he loved died at the hands of a murderer won't make it any easier on him.

What is the deal with Rosenstein playing the murderer in my dream? I assume it is because I had seen him at the police station. If I had met any other professors coming out of the police precinct last night, they would've played into my visions as the killer of Rhonda and Penny instead. But how weird is it to see one of my favorite people playing the bad guy at the university?

It is so disconcerting that it makes it even more frightening. It is like having a dream where sweet baby bunnies eat you alive. Werewolves would be scary, but being ambushed by carnivorous bunnies would be terrifying.

It's simply wrong.

But there is an ounce of truth in any vision. The murderer might very well be a professor or employee of the university. The murders were a long time apart, but they follow the same pattern. It might help clear Martin's name to confirm that the same person murdered Rhonda and Penny. That would exonerate Martin entirely.

I wish I knew what Rosenstein told the police. I consider calling him to discuss it with him. There is a chance his information is the missing link. Besides, it wouldn't hurt to get another person's input.

Graduation is in ten hours. The information I need will require some highly skilled computer archives work, too. Luckily, I know just the man for the job.

Chapter 12

Pulling on a thicker T-shirt, I pad out to the living room. Dusty leans against the counter, talking to Daddy while he scrubs an iron skillet. I reach out and tug on Dusty's sleeve.

"Good to see you up." Dusty lowers his eyebrows. "You need to get some breakfast in you."

I gesture toward the glass door. "Can I talk to you for a moment?"

"Sure."

Dusty slides the door closed behind us as we step out onto the patio. "What's up?"

"Is Miles still working with you?"

Dusty makes a scoffing noise. "Sure, he is. Why?"

"I need something checked out as quickly as possible."

Dusty crosses his arms. "It's Saturday."

"I know, Dusty. But I think I may be able to clear Martin's name. The problem is there are only ten hours until the graduation ceremonies."

He rubs the red stubble on his face as he laughs. "Dang, you don't ask for much."

"Come on. If it were me, you would want Martin to do everything possible to help."

"Lord, you can be a pain. I will try to get in touch with Miles, but I will not make any promises. It's not fair to put a time limit on research, and especially not when you are calling for it on a Saturday."

"Thank you, Dusty. I really appreciate it."

He holds up a hand. "Thank me after we're able to help. Like I said, no promises. What are we researching?"

I have an instinctive mind for litigation. I always cut directly to the root of the matter. "I need the Rhonda Riley and Penny Trickett case files. Rhonda did not commit suicide. Someone killed her. I'm sure if we cross the names involved in her investigation with Penny Trickett's murder, we will be able to identify the real killer."

"Rhonda's case file might be sealed, and Penny's might only be partial at this point."

"Are you telling me Miles can't do it?"

Dusty screws his face up as if to indicate I have lost my mind. "We are talking about Miles. He can access anything he wants. I'm just a little slow to follow how you concluded Rhonda was murdered, and that it was by the same person who killed Penny. Those seem like two huge leaping assumptions, and before I ask Miles to burn a day off, I would like to understand."

"The same person committed the two murders. If Martin wasn't involved in Rhonda Riley's murder, he couldn't be involved in Penny's murder."

"How do you know the murderer is the same person?"

I had hoped that Dusty wouldn't ask that question. Which is stupid of me. Of course, he would ask probing, uncomfortable questions. That's Dusty's nature.

"I had a dream, and the killer was the same in both dreams."

Dusty blinks. "Really? Who is the killer?"

I shake my head. "It was just a dream. Not a vision. But I know that if we can cross-reference the information between the two murders, we *will* identify the killer. More importantly, we can confirm that the police never should have arrested Martin."

"Too bad you haven't developed your skill better. It sure would be useful now if you could simply visualize the killer's face."

I sigh deeply. "Would've, could've, should've... So sue me, I decided to become a lawyer instead. I know that is the utmost disappointment to you."

Dusty laughs so hard that his round cheeks block most of his eyes. "You're a hot mess, April."

Like I haven't heard that my entire life.

We separate as we reenter my apartment. Dusty walks to my room as he pulls out his phone to call Miles, and I mosey into the kitchen to make small talk with the rest of the family and pick at the breakfast leftovers. It is a celebration in my honor, after all.

"Tammy isn't coming for graduation?" Mama asks.

She refers to my roommate for the last year and a half. Tammy still has another year in the nursing program.

"No, ma'am. Tammy's fiancée took her camping this weekend."

"Speaking of fiancées…"

I don't even bother to look in Daddy's direction. "Given that we already have one broken engagement and one divorce in the family, I think I'll wait and get it right."

"Don't be dragging me into this. Besides, Barbara and I were never engaged." Chase refills his coffee cup.

"If you two weren't engaged, the only thing you were missing was a ring," I point out.

Chase leans against the counter. "It was missing a little bit more than a ring." He blows the steam from above his mug. The conversation is over.

"Would you care to elaborate on that?" I never tire of asking my brother about him and Barbara. One day he will have to tell me.

"Nope."

Granny changes the subject. "Tell us about your new job."

"You mean my dream job. Master, Lloyd, and Johnson is one of the largest firms in the Southeast. This year, they only had two entry-level positions, and over six hundred candidates applied."

"That's impressive," Nana kicks in.

"I know, right? Lord knows I earned it by finishing in the top five percent of my class. Still, until I actually land the job offer, anything can happen."

Daddy leans back in his chair. "What sort of lawyers are they?"

"It's more about their client base, Daddy. They handle the

businesses and the personal affairs of hundreds of entrepreneurs in the greater Atlanta area. Mergers, acquisitions, taxes, estate planning, and nondisclosure agreements—they are a discreet, one-stop personal legal team for the movers and shakers of the Atlanta business world."

"Sounds shaky, all right," Daddy grouses.

If nothing else, Daddy is consistent. With Uncle Howard just a few years from retiring, I know Daddy holds out hope I will come home to take over Howard's law office… in Guntersville, the Podunk town I grew up in. I can't think of a more enormous waste of the seven years of education I labored so hard for and mortgaged so much of my future earnings to afford.

On the bright side, at least Daddy wants me to live nearby. That is sweet, though not helpful.

"I think it sounds exciting, Ralph." Granny puts her son in his place.

Mama sighs. "You knew from the time she could talk that she couldn't wait to get away from us, Ralph. I don't know why you think seven years from home would change her mind."

Mama has always taken me at my word. Unlike Daddy, she holds no unrealistic expectation of me moving back to Guntersville. Even though it is the truth, it sounds harsh the way Mama says it. I suspect she means for it to have a little bite to it.

I huff. "I'm not even going to be half a day's drive away."

Mama purses her lips. "No, but we'll all be busy. If we are lucky, we might see you at Christmas and Easter. At least until you get married, and then you will have to go to his parents' house."

Nana leans forward. "Viv, if you're going to be that ugly, she probably won't come visit at all."

"What?" Mama's eyebrows knit. "It's not like I'm saying anything you don't already know."

Granny clears her throat. Once she has everyone's attention, she raises her coffee mug. "Here is to a successful career for my beautiful granddaughter."

Everyone at the table, and Chase who is still sulking over at the counter, raises their coffee mugs in salute. An odd mixture of pride and sadness colors my emotions.

I hang out with my family in the kitchen for another hour to be a good hostess. Then I retreat to my bedroom to check on Dusty's progress.

Dusty sits at my desk with his laptop open. His nose is only a foot from the screen.

"How's it going?"

He jerks his head in my direction. "Oh, hey. It's actually coming along a lot quicker than I anticipated."

That is welcome news. I pull up an extra chair to sit next to him. "The same suspect in both cases?"

He shoots me a pointed glance. "No. Martin is the only suspect on record in Penny's case. As far as the investigators are concerned, they have their man for that murder."

Even though I feared that might be the case, it is devastating to have confirmation. Why wouldn't the police think Martin killed Penny? It is not uncommon for lovers to end a relationship in the worst way imaginable. One of her neighbors accurately fingered Martin as the man lurking outside Penny's house the night she was murdered. I would have also figured it was an open-and-shut case against Martin if I didn't know what I do.

"There was only one suspect of interest in the Rhonda Riley case. A Desmond Williams?"

"Desmond Williams? He was a guy Rhonda had a serious crush on in her tennis class. I didn't even know he was a suspect."

Dusty sighs. "He wasn't for long. The police were pretty determined to rule Rhonda's death as a suicide. But when a witness came forward about Desmond Williams, they did interview him. But Desmond didn't say anything that implicated him."

Desmond and I had worked on the same charity fund drive my junior year. It would be hard to imagine him as a killer even if he were angry. Then again, I could say the same thing about Martin.

This is all interesting, and I am sure Miles had to pull some major strings to obtain the information, especially on a Saturday. Not to be an ingrate, because I am grateful for the information, but I have no idea how this will help me free Martin.

"I'm sorry I wasted your time. I just knew there would be some common thread between the two murders."

"There is."

"There is?"

"Yes. The only thing is, I'm not sure what it means."

I twirl my fingers impatiently to get Dusty to pick up the pace.

"Both cases had one"—he holds up a finger—"witness come in on their own and give information that incriminated the suspects. Six years apart, the same person testified against Desmond and then Martin. Odd, right?"

Maybe?

Dusty continues, "Miles ran the name through a few neighboring states' databases, and bingo. He comes up as a registered sex offender in Arkansas. Something about sexually assaulting a drunk girl at a party when he was nineteen." He swivels his chair to face me. "When he moved to Alabama, he never registered as a sex offender. Probably because he wouldn't have been able to get his job."

Dusty drives me crazy with his long-winded stories. One of these days, he will cut directly to the chase on a question. Then I will think he is lying because he got to his point quickly. "Is he a pediatrician or an OB/GYN?"

"No." Dusty laughs. "Nothing that dramatic. But he is a professor at the school. A Professor Rosenstein? Do you know him?"

I stagger backward as if Dusty has slapped me—*hard*. My breathing is fast and shallow as the horror of the situation unfolds.

Suddenly, what I have struggled to remember the last two days locks into crystal-clear focus: the old visuals I had shoved deep into my mind. I wished to bury the awkward moment so I would never be required to address my actions.

I could have ended this and kept the girls from harm. Shame mixed with guilt weighs heavily on my conscience.

At the start of my sophomore year, Rosenstein and I discussed my abilities as a litigator. Now that the memory has dislodged itself, I can see, hear, and smell the day as it took place.

Friends might hear what happened and say, "How could you have known?" But I have never hidden behind vagaries. I guess I knew deep down inside, even though I didn't want to admit something was wrong.

The rest of Rosenstein's business law class had cleared out. I remained behind to talk to Rosenstein. I did this frequently.

There was a report of a tornado sighting outside the Tuscaloosa city limits. The wind picked up dramatically outside as tornado sirens began to wail in the background. I knew I needed to find shelter soon.

"We'd better get to the fallout shelter," I said as I watched the tree leaves fall eerily still.

"I've got a better place for us to kill the next hour," Rosenstein said.

An uncomfortable feeling wrapped around me as I parsed Rosenstein's comment. Time was of the essence, and you didn't mess around with tornadoes in Alabama unless you were dumb or had a death wish. "No, seriously, we need to go."

Rosenstein grabbed my wrist. His grip was loose yet stung my arm as if twenty bees had inserted their stingers simultaneously. My psychic senses jumped forward despite my barriers.

"Hey, buddy. Don't be getting all grabby with the merchandise." I tried to keep it light with the joke and allow him an easy out.

"Come on. You know you want to." Rosenstein curled his lip.

It was all I could do to restrain a nervous laugh. "Want to what?"

Rosenstein gestured behind him. "I've got a cot in my break room."

I shook his hand from my wrist and started for the classroom door. "Good for you, I suppose."

Rosenstein cut me off and grabbed my upper arm. Again, the wasp bites stung. "I'm serious. It will be fun."

I liked Rosenstein as a professor. But his antics, whether a joke or real, especially with imminent danger bearing down on us, enraged me. I pushed against his chest, and he stumbled back three complete steps. "I don't know what your game is, but if you touch me again, I'm going to carve out your spleen and kidneys."

Rosenstein studied me and then lowered his hands. "Geez, and here I took you for a girl who might enjoy a joke. I was kidding, you know."

I looked Rosenstein dead in the eye. "And I wasn't kidding. I'm very efficient at field dressing."

That encounter was what I hadn't been able to remember earlier.

It didn't surprise me that I had buried it. I'm not fond of things that I can't explain away. I'd buried it in this case because of my respect for Rosenstein's teachings. While he might have a royal-jerk side, I had learned a tremendous amount of information from the man. He had achieved a near-hero status with me.

Not excusing myself, but it is hard to find fault with your heroes.

"What's the matter with you, April?" The color in Dusty's face has leached out.

I am ashamed to tell him. If it was not absolutely necessary in order to facilitate Martin's freedom, I might not have. "This Rosenstein guy hit on me before Rhonda Riley and Penny Trickett. I just took it as an unwanted advance. I never thought it could lead to this nut job killing somebody."

Dusty grabs his phone and begins to dial.

"Who are you calling?"

Dusty presses the phone to his ear as he stares at me. "The police. Somebody needs to go pick this predator up."

I jump out of my chair and attempt to wrestle Dusty's phone away from him.

"What are you doing, April?"

I hear a voice on the other line. I stab my finger on the red button, and the line disconnects. I glare at my brother. "What do you think you are doing?"

His features pinch. "Watching my bat-crazy sister take my phone from me. What should I be doing?"

To be so bright, Dusty is so incredibly stupid. "Do you think they will release Martin because I come in and start telling them about a stupid dream?"

Dusty contemplates my question. "Well, it's true, so yeah."

I shake my head vehemently. "When it comes to the law, you must prove things. We must have facts."

He lifts his notepad. "The same man identified two different men on suspicious deaths. Come on, April. Police detectives are smarter than that. They just haven't noticed it yet."

I draw in a deep, steadying breath and attempt to explain as if I were speaking to a third-grader. "At this point, it's not considered corroborating evidence. It's simply coincidental facts unless we can get more information."

Dusty stretches his hands outward, palms up. "How in tarnation can we get anything more concrete in the time frame you're trying to hit?"

"I have a plan, but I'll need you and Chase helping me." I wait until I have his full attention before I pose my question. "Will you help me?"

"I don't know, April. I'm all about helping a friend, but this is starting to sound dangerous."

I shake my head. "Nope. It will go smoothly if everybody does what they need to do."

Chapter 13

My brothers and I park outside Rosenstein's single-story red brick house. He doesn't appear to be home.

A woman jogs by in a running outfit that leaves little to the imagination. "I like that. What do you guys think?"

Chase guffaws. "I'm not going to tell my kid sister what I think about that outfit. She'll tattle on me, and then I'll have Mama kicking my butt."

Rosenstein drives up in his black Camaro. We watch him enter his house, unaware of our vehicle. So far, so good.

"Now what, mastermind?" Dusty teases.

"I need a believable pretense for dropping by," I explain.

"You could ask to borrow something?" Dusty offers.

I roll my eyes. "Dusty, he lives half a mile away from my apartment. He won't believe that."

"It will if he is the only person you know for half a mile?" Dusty sulks.

"For Pete's sakes," Chase complains. "You said he is one of your favorite teachers. You're graduating. It wouldn't be unexpected for you to buy him a bottle of wine and tell him how much you appreciate him. It's just what friendly people do."

Dusty and I stared at Chase in amazement.

He arches his eyebrows. "What? It should work."

"You're a freaking genius," Dusty praises Chase and extends his fist to the back of the car, which Chase bumps with his fist.

That is the thing about Chase. I usually assume he isn't paying attention to anything unless it is a hunting or sports magazine. Then he drops a bit of logic on me that is darn near brilliant. It always leaves me scratching my head, wondering why I hadn't thought of it first.

Dusty drives us to a liquor store in the strip mall just down the street. I hustle in and select a fancy bottle of Merlot.

Nobody speaks as we pull back into position in front of Rosenstein's home. The tension in the car is palpable. Despite the air conditioning running on high, tiny beads of perspiration collect on my scalp. Dusty, in the driver's seat, shifts to say something. I cut him short.

"This should be easy, but I want to ensure we're all clear." My eyes scan the back of the car. All the color has drained from Chase's usually tanned complexion, and he has a sheen of sweat on his forehead. "I'm just going to go in, as an old student showing her gratitude, and as soon as I'm in there, I'll call you when he is opening and serving the wine."

"What if you can't? What if you cannot get to your phone without drawing attention?" Dusty asks.

Fair. But I can't afford to borrow any trouble. If I consider the possibility of being unable to call my brothers, I may lose my nerve. "There won't be any problem. People look at their phones all the time. He won't think anything of it. Just make sure to put your phone on speaker and mute it. Then make sure to record the whole conversation."

Chase shakes his head in disgust. "This is a stupid plan. You don't even know if we'll be able to get a decent recording."

"Your recording is just backup, Chase. I will be recording with mine too. You both must listen to know if I need help and when he confesses. More importantly, I want to know that there is a second recording if something happens to my phone."

Chase grabs the back of both bucket seats and pulls himself forward. "Don't think I don't understand what you mean about something happening to your phone, April. My kid sister sitting down with someone we suspect of killing two girls in cold blood? I can't believe I'm going to just let this happen. This plan is stupid."

"Don't be so dramatic. What do I have to be afraid of?" I favor both my brothers with a smile.

"Well, if you are correct, a murderer," Chase grouses.

"But you two will be listening in and hear everything."

Chase shakes his finger at me. "And that's another thing. Why do you have to wait until you're inside his house to call us? Why can't you call us now so we can make sure the phones are working properly?"

Bless it. My jaw drops and my mouth opens as I stare at Dusty. He offers me a chagrined shrug. That's two logic bombs in a row from Chase. Maybe we should call the whole excursion off. At this rate, I might be struck by lightning on the way to the door.

"I got this," Dusty says as he gestures for me to give him my phone.

I try to shake off the willies as I hand my phone over. "I have the advantage anyway, Chase."

"How's that?"

"Unlike Penny and Rhonda, I know Rosenstein is a monster. And even better, he doesn't know that I know."

"Yeah, I hear you, but I still think you are so full of crap your eyes are turning brown."

Dusty hands me my phone. I grab the bagged bottle of Merlot around the neck and open the car door. "Love y'all."

"Holler, and we'll be there," Dusty says.

"Be careful," Chase says.

I push the car door closed and stare at Rosenstein's house. I'm ready to do this. Somebody needs to bring the Rosensteins of the world down, and I'm the woman for the job.

Full of purpose, I stomp up his walkway onto his porch. My finger halts an inch from the doorbell. An icy cramp twists my stomach and threatens to turn me inside out.

Just butterflies, April. It's not a supernatural energy source. You're only nervous.

By sheer willpower, I poke my finger at the doorbell. I wait for

Rosenstein.

I seem to wait for an eternity. The oppressive humidity of the late-spring day envelops me in a cocoon of heat. It deadens all sounds in the neighborhood, save for the large bumblebee ambling along the tops of some daisies in desperate need of watering.

He must be too busy to answer his door. Bummer. I finally come to my senses and lose my nerve. What do I think I'm doing? This is such a bad idea.

I turn to leave, and the door pops open.

Rosenstein frowns at me and tilts his head to the left. "April?"

Smooth, April. Make it smooth. "You didn't think I was going to leave town without saying goodbye to my favorite professor, did you?"

"Wow." He makes an odd noise that is part grunt and part chuckle as he steps back from the door. "I had no idea. If I had known I would have company, I would have picked the place up."

I can barely bring myself to step over the threshold. The moment I do, the sense of doom makes me regret it.

Tremendous negative energy assaults my senses. Dark, thick, oily energy imprints attack me. I will never be able to scour this evil imprint from my mind.

"I hope you like Merlot." I hold the bottle out for his inspection.

Rosenstein bites his lower lip, and the creases around his eyes deepen. "Yes." His tone is cautious and halting.

"Oh, my goodness." I feign embarrassment. "You have company —a lady—I should have called first." I whirl around as if to leave. I would be lying if I said I don't hope he wants me to go. After feeling the sickening energy in the house, I doubt my ability to maintain the ruse.

"No!" His hand grips my upper arm, and complete darkness flashes before my eyes as the wasps sting me like years earlier during the tornado warning. "It's just such a surprise. I'm truly honored."

I extend the bottle toward him again. "Well, as I was saying, I'm not exactly a wine connoisseur, so I hope this is acceptable."

"I'm sure it will be great. I am truly blown away that you thought about your lowly old professor, as busy as you must be." He leers at me with such a hungry stare that I feel naked.

"I'm surprised you feel that way. I thought you knew that your sage advice convinced me to go to law school. Without that direction, I don't know where I would be."

"I'm glad it helped."

"You are a lifesaver, Professor Rosenstein." I admit I'm playing it a little too cute. But I want him to feel at ease. Even though watching him delight in my compliments repulses me, it lays the foundation for securing the confession I need.

Rosenstein stares at the floor before commenting. "You give me way too much credit, April. You would have found your way on your own if necessary."

I shrug and hold out the bottle for the third time. "If you say so. But either way, I hope you enjoy this in good health."

"I would enjoy it more if you would share it with me."

"I would love to, but my family is visiting for my graduation. I have to get back to them."

"Not even one drink for old times' sake?" He does his best sad puppy impersonation.

My repulsion transforms into guarded optimism. I barely conceal my excitement. With Rosenstein's elevated level of cynicism, he should have seen right through my snare. But he is walking willingly into the trap.

I blow out an exasperated breath. "I suppose I have time for one. A little one."

He smiles, but it does not reach his eyes. His stare is sharp and attentive, like a predator close to cornering its prey. "Make yourself comfortable, and I'll open the bottle."

I saunter to the sofa. "Please be quick. My parents are waiting."

"This will be over before you know it." Rosenstein disappears into the kitchen.

I pull out my phone and see that I somehow disconnected my brothers when it was in my pocket. "Fudge nuts," I grumble as I try to call them back. Nervous sweat tracks down my side from my underarms.

"Come on now," I whisper as I dial Dusty's number and press the record button. I set my phone face down on the coffee table in front of me and try to slow my heart rate.

Rosenstein's voice startles me as he reenters the room. "Lucky for us, you got a Merlot. Some people think they need to be chilled, but I'm of the mindset they are best at room temperature. Seeing you are in a hurry, it works out for us."

I stand to meet him and extend my hand for one of the glasses. He short-arms the glass on his left. I purposely reached across his body for it.

Acting like he doesn't notice me, he places the drink on his right into my hand and sits on the sofa across from where I stand. The move is so expert it gives me chills. How many times has he done this in the past? With his practiced degree of smoothness, it is hard to imagine that it has only been twice.

"I heard through the grapevine that you are striking out for the big city of Atlanta."

Another chill runs through me. The offer in Atlanta just came through last week. I have not talked to Rosenstein about my destination. Knowing what I now know, I don't want to think about why he might have been interested in where I will be living in the future.

"That's the plan. Of course, if a better offer comes in the meantime, I'll have to entertain that as well."

Rosenstein takes a sip of his wine and makes a smacking sound with his lips. "It must be nice being young and female. You have hundreds of options. It's as if the world is a huge buffet, and it's always young ladies eat for free night."

Wow. I'm amazed at how many hours of intensive counseling would be required to unpack all the latent hatred for women underlying his comment. How have I not seen this sooner?

I smile sweetly. "And here I thought it was a man's world."

Rosenstein's gaze traces from my feet to my chest. "It is in the natural world. When you strip away the thin veil of civility the courts impose, it is still very much a man's world."

It is time to make my move. I steel myself for the battle. To motivate me, I focus on what Rosenstein has stolen from Martin, Rhonda, and Penny. "Is that your goal, Professor Rosenstein? To strip away the civility of the world?"

He appears genuinely hurt by my question. Acting skills, or shock that I'd stand up to him? "Is that what you think, April? Do I seem that uncivil to you?"

"No." That is the truth. Except for the single incident I buried in my memory, Rosenstein has been one of the most civil men I have ever known. "But sometimes the worst people in the world are the most conscientious to never draw attention to themselves."

Rosenstein takes another sip of wine as he watches me over the rim of his glass. "You should try it, April." He nods his head toward me. "You would appreciate the taste—not too sweet, not too bitter. It reminds me a lot of you."

His statement sends a jolt through my brain. This interaction is more up close and personal than I bargained for.

He will never take the bait if he senses I am on to his crimes. The wine that gained me entry to his lair so easily has too quickly become a liability. I press the glass to my lips, pretending to sip. I smack my lips like he did. "Hmm... I'm not sure I've ever developed a taste for red wine."

"Nonsense. It's much easier on the palate than white wine."

What is in my glass might be smooth on the palate, but it would play havoc with my brain. From my earlier dreams, I know there is more in my glass than just wine.

I must keep the conversation going. I am closer to recording Rosenstein inadvertently saying something that ties him to the murders than I ever dared to hope. Now that I'm this near to my goal, I am concerned about the layout of his house. The last thing I need is for Rosenstein to escape after I coax a confession out of him.

I still feel uneasy that my covert mission is going too well, and it will blow up in my face soon. What if I can't get him to confess? Rosenstein has eluded conviction for his crimes this long due to a lack of sharing personal details of his life and a healthy dose of cynicism.

My doubt evolves into fear as I convince myself that, rather than admit his crimes, he will simply strike me dead at any moment.

I was overly optimistic to believe Rosenstein would neatly confess to the murders of Penny and Rhonda while I record the conversation. The idea that my brothers sitting in a car across the street could be my cavalry... Well, that seems even more ignorant now that I sit in Rosenstein's lair.

Now my grand entrapment of Rosenstein is "stupid," to borrow Chase's eloquent labeling. At the very least, my plan is more likely to fail than succeed. Which spells mortal danger for me.

"I always thought of you as an exceptional young woman, April. It means a lot to me that you came by today. It's as if things have come full circle. We can take care of unfinished business."

There is little doubt in my mind about what unfinished business he means. The strength of conviction I'd felt earlier must have been false bravado because I do not feel remotely brave now. "Oh, Professor Rosenstein, you probably tell all the girls that."

His eyes narrow as he studies me with the intensity of a hawk sizing up a rabbit three hundred feet below it. "Why are you here, April?"

My heart catches in my chest. Once again, Rosenstein has beaten me to the punch. I didn't prepare for his pointed question. "To say thank you to the professor who helped me find my calling in life."

Rosenstein leans back in his chair. "A thank-you card and a gift certificate to the local diner would have accomplished the same thing."

Every pore in my body leaks sweat, and tears collect on my eyelids, threatening to spill over. What did I think would happen when I came into Rosenstein's home alone? This isn't it. It is as if he knew my exact plan. Rosenstein regards me with restrained interest like a spider watching a moth struggle in its web.

Or is that a construct of my mind? Rosenstein might not suspect anything other than a long-time student has come by with a gift of wine. What is so unusual about that gesture of goodwill?

Due to Rosenstein's pointed questions, the sedative from the wine coating my lips, and the intrinsic evil coursing through this house, I make a snap decision. I must leave. I am in way over my head.

"I needed to make sure you know how much I appreciate you." I gesture over my shoulder toward the door. "I need to get back to my parents now."

"I still remember the day you threatened to field dress me." His voice is low-pitched and icy-cold.

I laugh, trying to lighten the atmosphere. "As I recall, you started that by being grabby."

He looks me up and down again in that cold, calculating manner, causing me to cross my arms protectively.

"You haven't been listening. Natural law says I can have anything I can overpower."

Hatred for this man suddenly blooms to unfathomable dimensions. How did I not see Rosenstein for the monster he is when I first met him?

He gestures. "You really should finish that Merlot. It'll grow on you. Help you relax." He smiles, exposing his teeth. "Trust me. It'll be better for you if you are relaxed."

Then the worst happens. "Is that what you told Penny and Rhonda?" slips out of my mouth.

That smacks the smile from Rosenstein's face. He leaps across the coffee table. His hand scrapes down my arm as I roll off the sofa to avoid his attack.

He is on his feet and grabs at me as I scramble around the table. I dart behind the sofa closest to the kitchen, realizing too late that Rosenstein has positioned himself between me and the doorway.

I can try my luck with the kitchen, but I don't know if there is a back door I can escape through.

"Maybe I made a mistake by using the barbiturates. Awake is a lot more exciting." Rosenstein favors me with an exaggerated shake of his shoulders. "It really gets the blood pumping. Doesn't it?"

"You are sick."

"You haven't seen sick yet, baby, but you're about to."

I reach into my back pocket for my phone. The cavalry is one "help" away. Mother of Pearl, my pocket is empty.

Sighing, I eye my phone on the table at the sofa's edge. Exactly where I left it.

Rosenstein considers my hand motion to my back pocket and follows my eyes to the coffee table. He picks up my phone and taps the screen. "Dusty Snow—your brother who writes those hack ghost books." He tosses the phone back onto the coffee table. "I guess we'll have to make this a quickie. Too bad. I was optimistic I could take my time."

Now, the kitchen seems like an excellent idea. I pivot and break into a sprint through the doorway. I hear Rosenstein fast on my heels.

I grab the doorknob as I crash into the back door. The knob doesn't turn.

"It's too early to leave. We haven't even had playtime yet."

Locked. It is a keyed deadbolt, too. Without the key, I'm not going anywhere. At least not out the back door.

I pivot to assess the situation. Rosenstein blocks the doorway between the kitchen and the living room. He has straightened to his full height, and I realize he is a bigger man than I thought. Bowling him over probably won't work, even if I am driven by fear and a strong survival gene.

"You really should try the wine. There is no need to fight the inevitable. It's going to happen whether you fight or not. Then it will all be over, and the sweet pain will be no more."

"If you think you're going to take me down, you better pack a lunch, you twisted freak, 'cause it's going to take you all day." I stall as I scan the counter for any weapon I can use. Why couldn't he have a knife block like other adults? "Win or lose, I guarantee I will be taking one of your eyes or a couple of testicles with me."

The corners of his lips twitch up. "Frisky—I love it. This is so much more exciting without the drugs."

My options are terrible and poor. I can hope to stall until my brothers decide to crash the door, or I can run down the hallway to the right of Rosenstein and hope there is some way to escape out of one of the rooms. Both options bite, but stalling seems like the best choice at the moment.

"So, I'm right. You killed Rhonda and Penny," I continue.

Rosenstein leans against the threshold and crosses his arms as if monumentally bored. "Maybe, maybe not. It won't much matter to you in a few minutes anyway."

My confidence plummets with every passing second. "Seems like there's no danger in you telling me the truth now."

"April May Snow, you think you're so smart."

Why have I not thought of that before now? The wine bottle could be my ticket. The wine bottle in the center island will be my weapon.

"Did you kill both of them here?" I know he did. The place reeks of terror.

His eyes hood over as he shakes his head. "You're still asking questions as if you'll be able to tell someone."

There is my confirmation. I will get only one shot to run to the island, grab the wine bottle, and strike Rosenstein. If I am too slow or double-clutch the bottle, I will die.

"I know you killed Penny because she was pregnant with your child, but why kill Rhonda?"

"I didn't mean to kill Rhonda. It was an accident. She was my first 'date,' and I put too much sedative in her wine." He shrugs. "Live and learn, I guess."

I say a little prayer and break for the island. I focus on the bottle, but I see Rosenstein lurch toward me.

I snatch the neck of the wine bottle and continue in a circular motion toward Rosenstein. He raises his arm to block me as I swing the bottle full force into Rosenstein's jaw. There is a distinct cracking noise as his jawbone breaks, shifting grotesquely to the side.

Rosenstein clutches the top of my blouse and shoves me backward. I swing the wine bottle again, striking him across the forehead.

The bottom of the bottle explodes, sending shards of green glass and a purple plume of liquid into the air.

My back slams into the wall, crushing the wind out of me. The wall's wood frame creaks from the impact. I still hold the broken wine bottle around the neck by some miracle.

I shove the jagged bottom into Rosenstein's ribs. He screams in agony, so I twist the bottle for good measure.

Undeterred, Rosenstein backhands his fist across my face. Every filling in my mouth vibrates like a tuning fork as a wave of overwhelming dizziness threatens to send me to the floor.

No, April. You can't black out. You must finish this fight.

I jab the wine bottle into Rosenstein's neck. Blood jets from the wound, and I think, just maybe, he will let me go and I can stumble out the front door. Once outside, my brothers will come to my aid.

Instead, Rosenstein grabs me in a bear hug with a grunt. His wild eyes are inches from mine. I have the terrifying realization this will be a fight to the death. His rage-fueled adrenaline dump has him focused on the solitary goal of killing me. He will not stop until I am dead or he has bled out.

Rosenstein lifts me off my feet and squeezes the air out of me. He body slams me onto the linoleum floor, and his entire weight crashes on my rib cage.

The scream of pain that escapes me sounds inhuman. For a second, the pain is so sharp I wish I would pass out to bring it to a swift end.

"Stupid girl. Cut me? Cut me! I'm going to make you eat that bottle." He roars with a gurgling voice.

He yanks the bottle from my hand, and I don't even care. I hurt too much to worry about the stupid bottle anymore. Rosenstein has ruptured something in my chest. I'm dying anyway.

Breathing is an impossible feat. Even if I could, the prospect of the pain that is sure to go with inhaling scares me as bad as suffocating.

Rosenstein grabs me around the jaw. His thumb and forefinger dig in, forcing my mouth to gape. I twist weakly, but there is no escaping his iron grip.

The jagged dark-green shards approach my lips. "Open wide."

I grab Rosenstein's forearm, slippery with the red mist spurting from his neck wound.

The bottle nears my lips, and I push harder. Malevolent images flow from Rosenstein's consciousness to my mind. My strength wanes, and I know I am losing the battle. I am about to die a horrible death.

In desperation, I bring my knee up violently. Nothing. I don't even connect with Rosenstein's back.

I pant with short, shallow breaths and continue an ineffective struggle to hold Rosenstein's arm up, the jagged edges of the bottle pushing toward my face. I turn my head to buy a few more precious inches.

Arching my back, I push with all my strength. My effort earns me a few more inches of clearance from my face, and Rosenstein's brow creases with the first hints of concern.

The momentum is turning in my favor.

I labor to catch my breath as I hold his arm in place. His neck wound is no longer a small spray. A steady flow spills freely onto my fractured chest.

I must roll over to earn some leverage. Realizing this might be my last best chance, I take a deep breath, lock my ankle outside of Rosenstein's ankle, and twist my body to the right.

Everything slows as I roll with momentum and reach my right side. I remain balanced on my side, unable to finish the roll, while Rosenstein struggles to stay on top of me. His facial features are a caricature of concern. His expression might be humorous—if we weren't locked in a Mortal Kombat deathmatch.

I don't know where the last bit of power comes from, but I feel it gathering. I scream a rebel yell and throw all my weight against the inside of his thigh. Sweet victory, my stomach rolls onto his kneecap as he loses balance. Quick as a rabid raccoon, I claw upward vigorously until I straddle his stomach.

My face is within inches of his now pasty-white face. I'm no doctor, but Rosenstein should be less concerned with me and a lot more worried about the slash on his neck that is bleeding him out.

His eyes widen as I lock my knees into his armpits. With all the adrenaline surging through my body, I must get rid of the broken bottle. If I hold it too long, I will finish Rosenstein off.

I push against his chest and stand.

As I swing my leg over his chest, he grabs my foot and twists, threatening to bring me to the floor. I yank my foot free from his grasp and stomp on his hand. He emits a weak grunt of pain.

"Stay down if you know what's good for you." I shake the bottle at him.

Rosenstein doesn't follow directions very well. For a half-dead man, he still moves quickly. Before I can react, he rolls onto all fours and grabs the center island to try and pull himself up.

I don't like it, but he hasn't left me with any choices. I kick him in the ribs as hard as I can, and he pops up off all fours, falling into a fetal position before cradling his sides.

Okay, I like it a little.

It is poetic justice, considering what he has done to my ribs.

I'm not going to claim to be the most brilliant girl in the world, but I will say that my sense of timing is excellent. It is time I get the heck out of Rosenstein's house, by my estimation. I don't need to give him a chance to recover, and I'm too tired and sore to go another round with him.

I run as quickly as I can manage in my injured state. I throw open the door, hit the screen door, and jump off the porch. Both doors of Dusty's car open simultaneously. I continue running toward the vehicle as Dusty and Chase trot through the front yard.

"Where were you!" I scream at my brothers with an accusatory tone.

We pull up inches short of one another, where both my brothers' faces change from concern to horror. Chase examines my bloodied shirt.

"Are you cut? Shot? Where?" His hands glide across my shirt.

I slap his hands out of the way. "Don't touch my ribs. The blood isn't mine. Why didn't y'all check on me?"

"I wanted to. Dusty said you would call when you were ready."

"You put us in an impossible situation, April. If we came in too early, we would blow your opportunity to find out what Rosenstein was up to," Dusty pleads.

It isn't fair, but I don't care right now. I punch Dusty in the chest. "I could have been murdered."

"But you weren't. All good?" Dusty raises his brow.

Chase pulls his phone out of his back pocket. "I don't care what you say. I'm calling the police now. They need to come and sort this out."

I slap myself on the forehead. "I forgot. Rosenstein is in there bleeding out."

Chase cuts his eyes toward me. "You want me to wait thirty minutes before we call the police?"

"No! Lord, no," I yell.

"I wouldn't mind taking my time if it meant that you wouldn't have to testify against him later," Chase continues.

"I'm gonna love testifying against him," I say.

Chapter 14

Despite his excellent idea, Chase defers to my request and calls 911, who confirms that the Tuscaloosa police and an ambulance will be to us momentarily. The dispatch requests that he stay on the line until the police arrive.

Chase hits mute and lowers his phone to his side. "They say they'll be here soon." He looks pointedly at me. "The ambulance, too."

"Should we go and check on him?" Dusty asks.

Chase squinches his face as if he bit into something terribly sour. "To do what? Stomp on his face?"

"To stop the bleeding. Geez, man, calm down already."

My life becomes a blur of red and blue lights strobing through a cloud of haze. I'm only partially aware as the first officer on the scene asks us questions. Most of the adrenaline has cleared my system, and I have half a mind to lie in the back of Dusty's car and nap until it is all over.

The EMTs exit with Rosenstein on a stretcher and speed him away with their siren blaring. One of the officers gives us the news that the EMTs were able to staunch the bleeding from Rosenstein's neck.

Oh, yay.

He has lost a tremendous amount of blood, but it appears he should survive. Survive until he has exhausted all of his appeals on death row.

Detectives Green and Cunningham appear and force me to recount everything I told the police officer about Rosenstein attacking me when I came to visit. Unfortunately, my thoughtfully designed plan to record the confession I coaxed from Rosenstein didn't work. Chase was right; the plan, in the end, was stupid.

Assuming Rosenstein survives our melee, it will be his account of the events versus mine.

Inside Rosenstein's house, I walk through the events of the attack. I do my best to describe the predatory tendencies of Rosenstein and tie the similarities of today's events with the circumstances of Penny and Rhonda's murders.

Cunningham tests my glass of wine with a "check your drink" strip. Spiked. That is a shocking surprise.

What is genuinely surprising is how Cunningham's attitude takes a complete one-eighty toward Martin as he examines the test strip. His enormous hands tremble as his upper lip curls with disgust. What his response lacks in eloquence, he makes up for with passion. "This is messed up, Carson. We have to get that kid released to his parents."

Detective Carson Green tries to reason with Cunningham that the DA won't appreciate a call on Saturday. The conversation ends with Green agreeing to see what they can do for Martin. There are no promises, of course.

Detective Green's car pulls away, and my brothers and I walk to Dusty's car. The engine rumbles to life. We sit trance-like as the air conditioning cools the beads of sweat on my face.

I break the silence. "I don't think we should tell Mama or Daddy about this."

"I'll second that," Dusty responds without hesitation.

"They would kill Dusty and me if they knew we let you go in there," Chase says.

"We'll need to get you a new shirt before we meet up with our folks." Dusty puts the car in gear. "Are there any clothing stores at that strip mall where we got the liquor?"

"There is a little boutique there. They're expensive, but it will do."

"I'll get it," Dusty says.

I draw in a ragged breath, and a sharp pain dances across my chest. "Man, my ribs hurt."

Chase exhales loudly. "I knew you were fibbing when that EMT asked if you were all right."

"I'm not missing graduation over a few bruised ribs. Rosenstein doesn't get to control my life like that."

Both brothers nod their agreement.

As the last of the adrenaline drains from my blood, I shake uncontrollably. Tears well in my eyes. I'm forced to breathe through my mouth as the inside of my nose swells. I did what I had to in Rosenstein's house, and I am proud I defended myself and came out the winner without the help of my brothers.

Still, the realization I was engaged in mortal hand-to-hand combat with a man who has experience killing women like me is nerve-racking. I should have been terrified. What the heck is wrong with me?

I lean forward and note my brothers' intense facial expressions. They look like they need an excellent PTSD counselor. It isn't the first time I have seen them like this. Nor is it the first time I have been the cause.

Most likely, it won't be the last time, either.

In addition to coming down from the excitement high of the fight with Rosenstein, it dawns on me that this might be the last hurrah for the Three Musketeers. Well, two musketeers and their crazy mascot sister.

It is sobering to consider this is it. After today, I will move to Atlanta, and the boys will continue without me. Today may make them grateful that I'm not returning to Guntersville, if nothing else. At least they won't have to worry about trying to keep me safe. Which has proved to be a nearly impossible task.

I will miss them terribly. I feel like I should have already dealt with all those emotions. But I haven't, and in my gut, I know Mama is right. When I move and start my new job, I will be busy, just like all of my family is, and the times we get together will be rare. I can't admit it to them because they would use it against me to convince me to stay, but I am apprehensive about being without their constant presence in my life.

Chase leans forward, laughing as he shakes his head. It isn't a funny ha-ha laugh, but more the hysterical laughter of a man on the edge of losing his composure.

"Man, I always knew you were mean, April. But if I had known you were capable of all that damage, I sure as heck would have thought twice about ever teasing you."

I snort a laugh. "You're just lucky I love you too much to open a can of whoop-butt on you." I quickly wipe away the tears that slip down my cheek.

"I'm grateful the only thing damaged is your shirt. Daddy would have kicked Chase and me out of the house for sure if you had gotten hurt on our watch."

"True that," Chase agrees.

We fall silent. I suppose we are all working through our shock.

Dusty pulls the car into the strip mall where we purchased the bottle of wine I used to cut Rosenstein open. He parks the car and pauses, his hand on the keys in the ignition. "So that Professor killed two other girls?"

I sigh deeply. "Yeah."

"And one of them was the ghost I felt in the storage bedroom at your sorority?"

"Uh-huh."

Dusty nods as he removes the keys from the ignition. "I wish I could've seen her."

"Best not. Rhonda's ghost is a mess. I wouldn't want you to see her that way." Thinking about her makes a lump form in my throat.

Chase clicks his tongue. "Do you think she will go to heaven now?"

This question from Chase is surprising on several fronts. First and most surprising is that even though Chase knows Dusty and I claim to have paranormal abilities, he usually ignores our discussions. Second, it is a surprisingly astute question.

What will happen to Rhonda now? Did she stay all these years to point at her killer in the rafting excursion picture on her bedroom wall? Why has she remained when Penny vacated the area immediately following her death?

One thing is for sure, looking for rules regarding the supernatural is enough to drive you crazy.

"I sure hope so, Chase," I croak.

He smiles. "Yeah, I think she will be free now. That's a good thing. You did a good thing today, April."

I lean back in the backseat to conceal the tears that fall uncontrollably. Yeah, I will miss my brothers something fierce, no matter how successful I become in Atlanta.

But anything worth having requires great sacrifice. Right?

Dusty opens the car door. "Let's see if we can find a blouse to match the one that you ruined."

Chapter 15

Since we are late coming home, our parents and grandmothers are too busy fretting about the compressed timeline to grill us effectively about why we almost missed the graduation ceremony.

My hair remains damp from my uber-fast shower as Mama pins my mortar cap, complete with *Atlanta or Bust* stenciled in pink on the top, at a smart angle on my head. It is surreal to realize the dream I have chased for the last six years is becoming a reality in less than two hours.

While Detective Green promised to do everything possible to free Martin for the graduation ceremonies today, getting a DA to act quickly on a Saturday will be a long shot. I'm hopeful, but I don't expect that miracle to come to fruition.

Martin labored as hard as I did to earn his degree. It is a shame that his parents won't be able to watch their son graduate with the rest of our class today.

But I can't be too sad about it. I did everything possible and probably risked more than most friends to help Martin. Knowing he will be exonerated in Penny's murder must be enough for today.

Hopefully, he can put his life back together and forget the awful thing that happened to Penny in time to take his position in DC. I expect wonderful things from Martin in the future. He has the right of it. He is one of the good guys, and the nation's capital could undoubtedly use more Martins.

"You look so smart," Mama comments as she straightens the shoulders of my gown.

"I am smart, Mama."

Mama smiles, but it doesn't reach her eyes. They are sad and liquid. "Yes, you are, baby."

Daddy enters my bedroom, making a show of checking his watch. "If we don't get a move on, they will have to mail her that juris doctorate."

"It still counts if they mail it to you, Daddy."

He raises his eyebrows. "I did not come into enemy territory so they could mail my daughter her degree."

I pat his shoulder as I pass by him. "Stop with the enemy territory, Daddy. You have a Bama graduate in the family now. You have to be neutral."

He follows me while grumbling, "Football season isn't going to be as much fun without someone to hate."

"Then hate Tennessee," I suggest.

"She has a point. Everybody hates UT," Chase says.

We separate at the auditorium, and the strange magic my family holds over me fades precipitously every second I am away from them. That is precisely why I am moving to a new city.

When I am on my own, I am April Snow, the bright, resourceful young professional who can handle any challenge and doesn't back down from a fight. By myself, I am disciplined, motivated, and ambitious.

In Guntersville, I am Dusty or Chase's kid sister or Viv and Ralph's daughter. There is always someone trying to explain why I should or shouldn't live my life in a particular manner under the guise of looking out for me.

It is sweet but unnecessary. I am more than capable of taking care of myself.

Besides, Atlanta offers countless financial opportunities for a motivated young woman like me. I will be a full partner at Master,

Lloyd, and Johnson within the next three years. Forget the fact that it usually takes ten to fifteen years for someone to make partner at the firm. I am a force to be reckoned with, and I plan to leapfrog anybody else they have vying for those positions.

My law professors filled my mind with the expectations for my new career. Expensive sports cars, two-thousand-dollar bottles of wine, and month-long vacations to Barbados are on the docket. Life is good, and it is only going to get more excellent.

None of that can materialize in Guntersville.

I'm debating if I prefer to own a house on Buckhead Lake or a convenient condo near the Georgia Tech campus when I notice a familiar face in my periphery.

It is hard to miss Detective Cunningham in the sea of average-sized men and women. This morning when Cunningham was questioning me, Dusty and Chase were by my side, and I didn't fully appreciate Cunningham's giant status. I wonder why he has come to my graduation.

Cunningham steps to the side, revealing Detective Green. Green and I lock eyes. He smiles and favors me with a thumbs up.

A thumbs up? I don't know him like that. It is odd he showed up at my graduation. Creepy even.

"I need to get to the front of the line, Snow. But I want to say thank you before I do."

I turn to the familiar voice, then jump, squeal, and embrace Martin. "How did you get out?"

His mouth is close to my ear. "You should know better than anybody how. You're the reason, April Snow. Without you, I wouldn't be here."

I drop my arms and continue to smile at him like a loon. "Green was able to talk a judge into coming in?"

Martin grins. "Nah, they needed to question me more about my timeline, and we're just making a stop on the way to the crime scene." He offers me a sly wink.

I wave in the direction of Cunningham, but he is looking at the stage. Who would think his heart is larger than his biceps? He might look scary, but he is all right in my book.

"Are your mom and dad in the crowd?" I ask Martin.

"You know it."

"And you will be at the party afterward?"

Martin's eyes scan the floor. "No. They have to get me back to the station by then."

"Why can't the detectives run you by the party?"

Martin's brow creases. He stares at me as if I have gone crazy. "It's just a party, April. Lord knows I have been to enough parties for one lifetime. It's not going to hurt me to miss one. But this?" He waves his hand at the crowd assembled in the basketball arena. "This is special. And this I owe to you."

My face flushes. "You are giving me way too much credit."

"No—no, I'm not."

"Mr. Culp, you must get to your seat. We'll be starting any second." A young professor puts her hand between Martin's shoulder blades, nudging him toward the stage.

"Don't you forget about me, April Snow. You give me a call someday from that corner office in Atlanta. You hear me?"

"You'll have to fly down from DC and visit me, too."

He doesn't answer me. Martin walks to the front, smiling at me over his shoulder. I watch until he takes his seat, where my view of him becomes blocked.

There is a hollowing in the center of me. The vast space once occupied by my crazy, fun-loving family, then temporarily filled by my sorority sisters and, most recently, my law school friends such as Martin, feels empty again.

The empty feeling aches and makes me so sad I nearly miss when they call my name. Walking across the stage, I hear Chase's voice boom, "Way to go, April!" above the clapping. He has never been much for social mores, and it brings a brief smile to my face.

As I sit with my juris doctorate in hand, I contemplate how I am no longer a resident of Guntersville, Alabama, nor a student at the University of Alabama. It is both exhilarating and scary. I only hope that I am ready for the challenge of the next stage of my life.

Who am I kidding? I'm April May Snow. I'm intelligent, tenacious, and educated. The rest of the working stiffs at Master,

Johnson, and Lloyd aren't going to know what hit them. Hotlanta, here I come!

THE END

April's story continues with,

Throw the Dice
Click here to get your copy.

Have you read the *Psychic Witch's Life* novel series? It is the continuation of the *Psychic Witch Hot Mess* prequel series.

Click to get your copies today!

Psychic Witch's Life are the April May Snow Guntersville Novels.

Foolish Aspirations

Foolish Beliefs

Foolish Cravings

Foolish Desires

Foolish Expectations

Foolish Fantasies

Foolish Games

Foolish Haints

M. Scott lives outside of Nashville, Tennessee, with his wife and two guard chihuahuas. When he's not writing, he's cooking or taking long walks to smooth out plotlines for the next April May Snow adventure.

Dear Reader,

Thank you for reading April's story. You make her adventures possible. Without you, there would be no point in creating her story.

I'd like to encourage you to post a review on Amazon. A favorable critique from you is a powerful way to support authors you enjoy. It allows our books to be found by additional readers, and frankly, motivates us to continue to produce books. This is especially true for your independents.

Once again, thank you for the support. You are the magic that breathes life into these characters.

M. Scott Swanson

The best way to stay in touch is to join the reader's club!
www.mscottswanson.com

Other ways to stay in touch are:

Like on Amazon

Like on Facebook

Like on Goodreads

You can also reach me at mscottswanson@gmail.com.

I hope your life is filled with
magic and LOVE!

Made in the USA
Monee, IL
31 January 2023

25835335R00073